The Story of Anna P,
As Told by Herself

The Story of Anna P,
As Told by Herself

by
Penny Busetto

First published by Jacana Media (Pty) Ltd in 2014

10 Orange Street
Sunnyside
Auckland Park 2092
South Africa
+2711 628 3200
www.jacana.co.za

ISBN 978-1-4314-1016-3

Cover design by publicide
Set in Sabon 11/15pt
Printed and bound by Creda Communications
Job no. 002183

See a complete list of Jacana titles at www.jacana.co.za

Time present and time past
Are both perhaps present in time future,
And time future contained in time past.
If all time is eternally present
All time is unredeemable.
TS Eliot, 'Burnt Norton'

Preface

I AM NOT SURE ANY MORE HOW I ended up here on the island. I think I came to see the ruins and forgot to go back. The local school needed an English teacher and I was asked to stand in until the Ministry in Rome appointed someone.

But that was twenty years ago.

I have lived all these years in uncertainty, knowing only that any day the real teacher may arrive. In the meantime a cheque has been deposited into my account each month. It is not much, but then I haven't had many needs except for paper and ink to carry on this endless dialogue with myself.

The islanders call me *l'Inglese,* the Englishwoman, although I have not spent more than a few months in England in my whole life. They are kind enough to me, but I am aware that they speak more slowly to me than they do amongst themselves, as if I were a slightly retarded child. I know it is out of kindness that they do it, yet I have wished at times that they wouldn't and that I could just be one of them.

I suspect that they are puzzled by me, that implicit in the name *l'Inglese* is a sense also of *la Pazza,* the mad woman, although they would never call me that to my face. I think I do not make much sense to them, simple as they are, but then perhaps I do not make much sense to myself either. I am always here, like them; I get up every day at the same time, breathe the same air, eat the same food, yet I have no common purpose with them. I have not tried to explain where I come from, and I think they would not understand if I did. To them Africa is what you can see across the straits on a clear day. It doesn't connect with an eccentric Englishwoman in any way. To their knowledge I have no past – or family either. I have sometimes wondered what the islanders would do if I died, as at some point I suppose I must.

I am always filled with a yearning for something I can't put my finger on or understand. At times the pain is so great that I wish I were a man and could pay a woman to hold me for a few hours, to make it pass. My body longs to be held and comforted, to know the warmth and softness of touch.

And after a while I began to realise that it doesn't make much difference whether one is a man or a woman.

I have on occasion, after payday at the end of the month, left the island and, in the anonymous back streets of a big city by night, found the courage to approach a woman and offer her money to spend the night with me. It is not about sex, you understand, although of course there is that too. But it is when the pain of being alone grows so great that it threatens to overwhelm me. We rent for the night, for the space of a few hours, a small room in a nearby *pensione* under the cynical scrutiny of the concierge and climb the dusty stairs to the small room. A high bed that must have belonged to someone's grandmother, a washbasin and bidet, a crucifix on the wall – the bare essentials for living and dying. From the walls come the groans and sighs of others like me who find the indifference of the universe too much to bear, who are trying to find temporary respite. Or perhaps not. Perhaps it is just about the bodily itch?

I have found a woman who suits my needs well enough. Sabrina she calls herself, although I am sure that is not her real name. The transaction is quick and shameful, and money changes hands – the price includes the room. She shows no interest in me, asks no questions. We slip naked between the sheets in the light that filters through the shutters from the street lamps. The understanding is clear. She is willing to share her body with me for a few hours, that is all. At first she felt she must perform, give me my money's worth. Now she just holds me close. Sometimes there is release. Sometimes just the holding is enough.

Sometimes when it is over I feel her eyes on me in the mirror as she tidies her hair and prepares to leave, but she never tries to breach the distance now that our bodies have separated. She works well on the level of bodies.

I catch the first ferry back to the island in the early light of morning, bundled up against the cold and damp. I watch the gulls swoop and dive in our wake, the first rays of sunlight reflecting off their wings as they rise, while we below are still caught in darkness and the mainland slips slowly off the horizon. I go straight from the harbour to school.

The island, you ask? Well, it's not much more than an extinct volcanic outcrop of rocks, with a tiny circular harbour nestled into its water-filled crater. The little village springs up around its sides. The roads are too narrow for even a Cinquecento to pass so you have to walk or take a Vespa to travel around. There is never enough water here. We collect and store rainwater in winter, but the summers are long and hot and there is never enough. Supplies have to be brought over by ferry in huge containers from the mainland.

There are two or three peaks that are not very high, but beneath the cliffs are deep half-submerged caves that have been hollowed out and shaped over thousands of years by the succeeding inhabitants of the island. The Romans bred moray eels in them. Sometimes they would throw a slave into the water for the entertainment of their guests, watch his flesh being torn from his limbs, the white bones exposed by the sharp teeth.

Pontius Pilate was born here, they say, the Roman governor who washed his hands of the whole affair with the troublesome Jew. He drowned himself in a river afterwards. And Giulia Livilla, sister of the emperor Caligula, died here in exile, alone, of hunger. I wonder about her sometimes, what she thought as she sat here at her window looking out across the waves towards Rome, when she realised that there was no longer any hope of return. Or did she keep on hoping until the very end?

Even Mussolini was exiled here in 1943 until Hitler's troops rescued him and set him up as a puppet dictator in Salò. I have seen a copy of his ration card. So much bread, so much sugar, so much butter each day, the little things of our lives. Did he have forebodings of his end a short time later? They hanged his body by the feet in Piazzale Loreto, you know, like Judas, upside down. And the people of Milan spat on his body and howled out their rage. One of the shadier incidents of the war. The heavy body hung there in the spring breeze. I have seen the documentary, the flickering images on the screen, the people of

Milan with fierce faces, hollow cheeks and sunken eyes etched with hunger, pain and fear from years of war.

1
Book of the Present

Here is a place of disaffection
Time before and time after
In a dim light.
                    TS Eliot, 'Burnt Norton'

Friday 19 October

As I hurry from the harbour to my classroom, the school secretary, Signor Cappi, stops me and hands me a letter. Without looking at it I push it into my briefcase. By eight am I am in front of the class of children, trying to explain the difference between the present perfect tense in English and the *passato prossimo* in Italian. Each of us isolated, encapsulated in his own world of meaning. Outside the classroom windows the island beckons to them.

The morning trundles on as usual and I try to put the letter from my mind, but I am aware of its presence pulling at me each time I get up and distance myself from it to write on the blackboard. The children are quiet, as if they, like the branches on the vines on this autumn morning, feel the sap ebbing in their limbs. They sit at their desks, separate, each absorbed in the slow inner functions of their organs, the secretions, the seepages, the rhythmic contractions and releases, the passage of sludge through the system. I see that it will not be much use to try to do any work with them unless their life forces can be quickened in some way so I devise a game, noticing as I do that Ugo is on the edge as usual. He stands holding his desk with two fingers, half turned from the others with his large frightened eyes, longing for inclusion yet fearing it at the same time.

At the end of the lesson I hold him back, a shy awkward boy who is struggling with the abstractions of schoolwork. He waits by the blackboard, a hint of panic in his eyes as he moves his weight heavily from foot to foot. I invite him to sit down, and sit near him. I can sense his fear, smell the nervous perspiration as it breaks out on his body.

– How are things going, Ugo?

He shrugs.

– How's everything at home? Your mother? Father?

His eyes move nervously across the desk and with his thick fingers he plays with a scrap of rubber from an eraser.

– Your marks in English are not very good. I suppose you know. How are you doing in your other subjects?

I wonder why I am subjecting him to this. It doesn't feel necessary and I am beginning to wish I could get out of it.

– Are there any problems?

I see his shoulders begin to shake. He pushes the chair back with his knees and stands up.

– *Debbo andare*, he says.

He stumbles out of the room.

I sit down at my desk, open my bag and pull out the letter. I examine the envelope carefully, official manila brown with *Polizia di Stato* printed in black across the top, and my name in sloping letters below. There is a red stamp, *Urgente*, across the side. I replace it in my bag and gaze out of the classroom window. From where I sit I can see out over the fallow fields behind the village where dry husks of corn lie untidy on the hard ground. A few vineyards straggle along the edges of the fields. The small sour grapes they yielded now lie fermenting in barrels beneath the houses. There is a sense of sadness in the island at this time of the year. The sea changes colour, becomes dark and opaque, and the first wild storms of winter keep the ferries from entering the harbour. The tables in the piazza where people sat eating and laughing until late are stored, piled up neatly in a back room for next summer. An unshaven man gazes out of a steamed-up bar window at the waves that crash against the harbour wall, then focuses again on the soccer results in the *Gazzetta dello Sport*.

I see Ugo again in the afternoon as I am walking home after school. He is helping at the vegetable stall in the marketplace, counting and weighing vegetables in a rusty old-fashioned hand scale. He sees me coming and withdraws to the far side of the square. I go up to the stall-keeper, a large muscular man with a shaven head in torn blue overalls and heavy boots.

– *Mi dica?*

I give him my order and, as he is putting it together, I comment that he is lucky to have his son working with him today.

– *Macchè! Non è figlio nostro* – his wife breaks in, a battered-looking woman with peroxided hair – *è figlio di mio*

4

fratello. Our nephew. *Capisce? Suo papà lavora a Milano.*

I thank them and pay.

I return to the tiny apartment I rent from Signora Bruna, a gaunt woman of indefinable age who runs her establishment near the harbour in the old part of town and lives next door. The entrance leads off an alley and up a steep flight of steps to my door. A large room with a kitchen table and two chairs in the middle and a bed against one wall. Uneven red flagged floor. A worn armchair before the deep shuttered window that looks out on to the rooftops and the sea beyond. A two-plate gas cooker. A sink. A fridge. A tiny bathroom. There is a sign on the back of the bathroom door that reads:

Rules of the house:
No television or radio.
No noise after 8 pm and before 7 am.
One hot bath a week. One cold shower a day
Rent to be paid strictly one month in advance on the first day of the month.
Thirty days' notice required.

My window overlooks the harbour sideways on. I have placed my armchair beside it so that I can note the time of arrival and departure of the ferries, the changes in shift of the *Carabinieri* and the *Guardie di Finanza*, the return of the fishing vessels, each year with less and less fish.

I climb the steep narrow staircase to my apartment and close the door behind me. I throw my bag on to the kitchen table, and as I do I remember the letter. I pull it out and examine it again. It is addressed to me.

Gentilissima Signorina
Anna P.
c/o Scuola Elementare Giosuè Carducci
Via Vincenzo de Luca
0427 Ponza

I turn it over. The address on the back is: *Polizia di Stato, Questura di Roma, Via San V.* I drop it on to the table and make myself a cup of tea, but while the kettle is boiling I pull the letter back towards me and tear it open with the end of my teaspoon. I draw out the single sheet of paper. I'm not sure why but I feel my heart beating.

It's just a few lines, from a certain *Ispettore* Lupo, at the police headquarters in Rome, informing me that I need to come to the *Questura* urgently and bring all my documents with me. He does not explain why. I neatly fold the page and return it to its envelope and put it on top of the fridge making sure to align it with the edge.

I take some birdseed off the shelf and feed my little songbird, my *cardellino*, in its cage, trying to put the letter from my mind. I bought it at a Saturday morning market in the capital a few weeks ago where it was on sale as a decoy for hunters. The bird is a fearful little thing, and I am not sure yet whether it can sing or not. It hasn't made a sound so far. Some do, some don't. I have hung the cage by the window in my room, from where it can see the hills and the sea.

I carry my tea over to the window and sit down in my armchair with my notebook and pen and my school bag. I have started writing to try to fill these interminable evenings that are now drawing in, growing darker and darker and colder. But first I correct the small pile of homework the children have left me and prepare my lessons for the morning. Tomorrow, with the fifth grade, we will look at the definite article, *the*. I think this must be the twentieth time I have repeated the same lesson. A whole generation of children has passed through my hands in the meantime. In a year or so their children will be old enough to come to my class. The parents have grown up, married, often left the island to find work elsewhere. Their children have been left behind with their grandparents to repeat the cycle.

I sip my tea and gaze out of the window over the rooftops at the island below.

I wonder what *Ispettore* Lupo wants.

The swallows are flying low, zigzagging, crisscrossing the sky in search of the millions of invisible insects that must also be flying low as the barometer drops. I know this means they will soon be leaving on their long migration south. Perhaps some will go all the way to the Cape of Good Hope. I straighten up in my seat to watch them, half in love with their speed, their concise precise movement, the way they twist their bodies at the last moment to avoid colliding with branches, masts, roofs, chimneys, and soar up and up into the sky.

Saturday 20 October
It is a cold rainy day, the first real autumn day of the season. After school I come home and read. Eggs and salad for supper.

Sunday 21 October
It is still raining.

Monday 22 October
School. Risotto with mushrooms.

Tuesday 23 October
This morning I am on playground duty at break. I pull a chair outside into the open air and sit in the shade against the classroom wall, steeling my eyes against the sharp sunlight, watching the children, ready to intervene if a fight breaks out, if someone grazes a knee.

They stamp and run and shout. The girls are playing in groups of twos or threes on the soft grass near the school building, imagining families and relationships, skipping and chasing each other. The boys, nearly all of them, are engaged as usual in a game of soccer on the sandy stretch of open ground behind the school building – they play football every break, usually with a ball made of a bundle of pages torn from the middle of an exercise book bound round and around with sticky tape.

My eye is caught by a movement on the ground at my feet. I bend down and see a wasp moving over an insect, a large moth. I can see the wasp holding it, see its abdomen connect and sting. The moth struggles then is still. I look up again. A few loners, or poorly coordinated boys, hang unhappily on the fringes of the game, unwilling to lose face by joining the girls' games but uncomfortable in the rough and tumble of the soccer match. I see Simone, small for his age, pale-faced with thick glasses held on with elastic around his head, pushing a toy car around on the dusty ground, making vrooming noises in his throat. I see Ugo standing nearby watching him, his back to the fence, with his arms outstretched and his hands gripping the diamond wire mesh as if he had been crucified. I wonder what it would take to make him breach the distance, what would persuade him to risk rejection and join Simone in his play. He doesn't often join in with soccer, and I am used to seeing him separate, but this time it is different. He looks afraid. I am uncertain whether to approach him or not, not wanting to worsen his fear or discomfort but reluctant to leave him there alone. I don't want to move out of my own solitude, but I find it almost impossible to just sit and watch. I wait a few minutes but, when nothing changes, I get up and slowly, as if taking a stroll, begin to walk around the edge of the improvised soccer field.

As I watch, I see Leonardo and Matteo break away from the soccer game and say something to Ugo. I see his eyes shift away from them, then his arms draw inwards and he pushes himself away from the fence. I see Leonardo laugh and shove his shoulder. I see Ugo's look of fear, his uncertainty. Leonardo pushes again and he stumbles, and now Matteo has shoved him from the other side and he falls, and I see the boys starting to kick his prostrate form. He does nothing to protect himself, he just lies there as the two boys kick him all over, and now the other children have noticed and are forming a circle around them, egging them on as the kicking continues. I run to the circle shouting, but the noise is so loud that no one hears me. I break through the ring of children at last and grab hold of

Leonardo's arm. He is red in the face and his lips are drawn off his teeth in what looks like a smile. There is sudden silence and the circle begins to disintegrate. I tell Leonardo and Matteo that I want to see them. They must wait outside the classroom door in silence until I come.

I make sure that everyone has gone before I turn to Ugo. He picks himself up self-consciously. I feel irritated with him; I wish he were not so pathetic, that he would defend himself, value himself a little. I help to dust him off. His face is scratched and bleeding so I take him to the bathroom and wash his hands and face. Some of the cuts are quite deep. I realise I am going to have to take him to the secretary's office to have the wounds disinfected and bandaged. It is something I do not want to do. I tell him curtly to follow me. Signor Cappi, the secretary, sits him down on one of the chairs reserved for visitors to the school and goes to the storeroom to fetch the first-aid box, then returns and sits on the arm of the chair and gently dabs at the boy's face, talking to him soothingly and kindly as he does so, probing ever so gently into how he got hurt. His eyes go from my face to Ugo's. The child does not speak but passively allows himself to be nursed. I am not sure what the procedure is but feel certain that I will have to make some kind of report at this point, to the headmaster, to the parents, to authority in general.

I return to the classroom where the two boys are waiting.

– So, Leonardo, what was that all about?

He looks at me sullenly, and then averts his eyes.

– *Niente*, he mumbles.

– That wasn't nothing. I saw you push and kick him.

– *Era colpa sua. Cercava guai.*

– How could it be his fault? He was just standing there watching.

The boy stares stonily at the wall. I tell him to go and wait outside, and then call in Matteo. He is a softer, more pliable boy, I know.

– *Allora, Matteo*, tell me what happened.

9

He bursts into tears. I watch the sobs racking his shoulders.

– *Non volevo, è che ci guarda sempre, e Leo m'ha detto di dargli una lezione. E mi dispiace.*

– Sorry? Yes, well sorry is good. Would you be prepared to say sorry to Ugo?

– *Si, Maestra.*

One at least is saved.

I send him back to his classroom. But I will have to deal further with Leonardo.

Outside, I watch the grub struggle then lie still as the wasp inserts its ovipositor into the flesh and begins to lay its eggs. Soon they will hatch and tiny maggots will begin to devour the living creature from the inside. It will die when they are ready to emerge into the world.

Wednesday 24 October

I am in class, setting up for the next lesson when one of the girls from the fifth grade knocks on the door and enters shyly.

– *Mi manda il Segretario. C'è una telefonata.*

I lock the door of the classroom behind me and walk swiftly along the dark echoing passage to the secretary's office. He gestures towards the receiver lying on the counter. I pick it up.

– *Pronto. Chi parla?* Who's there?

– *Qui è la Questura di Roma di Via San V.* This is *Ispettore* Lupo speaking. *Ha ricevuto la mia lettera di convocazione?*

My voice trembles slightly as I answer.

– Yes, I received the letter.

– *Perchè non si è presentata?*

I can't think of anything to reply. Why hadn't I gone to see him as he had asked? My mind is blank. A shiver of apprehension runs through my body.

– *Deve presentarsi immediatamente in Questura.* You must report to the police headquarters in Rome immediately.

– What is it about?

– *Lei lo sa.* You must come at once. You know why.

– No, I don't know. Please tell me.

– *Certo che lo sa.* You have received our letter.

I don't reply. His voice becomes mellifluous, persuasive.

– *Perchè non vuole venire?* Why don't you want to come? What are you hiding? *Che cosa nasconde?*

– I'm not hiding anything. Why do you need to see me? Can't you explain over the phone?

The tone changes at once.

– *No, deve venire in Questura di persona, con i documenti.* You must come here in person. With your documents. Without delay.

– I can't come now. I am busy.

He waits for me to continue. At last I manage to mumble:

– I'll come on Friday afternoon, after school. I can't come before then.

– *Va bene. L'aspetto venerdì. Ma mi raccomando, non manchi.* But I'm warning you. You'd better be there.

I replace the receiver carefully and softly in its cradle and return to my classroom.

Thursday 25 October

School. Home. I have a cheese sandwich for lunch.

At last I pull out some paper and my paints.

I clear the table so that I can work without worrying about knocking things over or messing them. I put down some sheets of newspaper and set out my paints and colours. For some time now I have been obsessed with painting self-portraits. I have hung them about my apartment and they now cover every surface and in places are doubled up even, since there is nowhere else to hang them: small ones, large ones, in oils, in inks, in watercolours. The eyes follow me constantly, watching, judging. They are not soft, there is no compassion in this gaze I turn on myself.

Today too I feel a need to paint a self-portrait, to capture something about myself that doesn't feel very clear to my understanding, some microscopic shift. I hold a small mirror in my left hand and paint with the fingers of my right, trying to trace the lines, the darkness and light that I see reflected. I have begun to know the shapes well. I work swiftly, the lines already so familiar to me, the deeply etched frown that pulls my eyebrows close to protect my eyes from the glare, the dark shadows under the eyes. This is the core of my face, of my portraits, that I paint again and again, often not bothering with the other features, which feel less distinct.

This time the colours run and blend in places and my expression comes out particularly dark and anxious-looking. I suddenly feel exhausted. I pack everything away and lie down on my bed, hoping to make time pass, hoping that it will soon be night and that I can end this day, which hasn't been a particularly bad day, so I am not sure why I am feeling so scratchy. I look at my watch. Only an hour has passed. It is only five o'clock. Three hours to go before supper. Six hours before bedtime. How am I going to fill this time?

I put my hands into my pockets in boredom. They are full of junk as usual. I pull out the contents and examine them dully. Amongst the crumpled tissues and odd coins I find a receipt. It is from a hotel in Rome. *Pensione Arcadia.* It is made out to my name. Strange, I have no memory at all of having been there.

I fall into a troubled sleep.

Friday 26 October
On Friday afternoon I take the 2.30 ferry to Anzio. The sun is hazy over the sea, high cirrus clouds filter and obscure the light but the glare is painful to my eyes. Spaces in between, transitions. I take the bus in rush-hour traffic, where bodies are stacked, piled into the little standing space and pressed up tight against one another. And after a while I feel an anonymous hand touch me, grope, then slide under my skirt. *La mano morta,* as they call it here, the dead hand. I try to move away but the disembodied hand follows me so I eventually get off in the square a few stops away from Via San V. and walk the rest of the distance to the *Questura*, my feet echoing on

the pavement. The rubbish bins, the *cassonetti*, are full and garbage is overflowing on to the pavement. Some of the bags have been torn open and orange peels and coffee grinds litter the ground. I stop breathing as I walk past, but it takes too long and when I am forced to take a deep breath the smell of decomposition fills my lungs.

Outside the building, tired-looking people hang around waiting, leaning against the iron railings or smoking nervously. It is impossible to distinguish the bystanders and informers from the plainclothes policemen, scruffy and unkempt, who wait with them, attempting to infiltrate their lives.

I go into the dusty drab shabbiness of the *Ufficio Stranieri* of the *Questura*, the immigration section, the high wooden counter at which lines of people wait, day in, day out, mostly immigrants hoping for a break, hoping that today, at last, all the documents they need will miraculously come together and the file will be complete and they will be given the *permesso di soggiorno* that will allow them access to the land of milk and honey, to the stability that makes possible memory and hope, which are so tenuous even here but impossible in their places of origin. Africa, Asia, Middle East, South America, Central America, Eastern Europe. Just about anywhere except for this small haven of privilege here where they are trying to find a space, a tiny harbour that will take them in and give them rest. A place that will allow them to collect themselves and their memories and aspirations and make a story, a narrative that will give meaning to their fragmented lives.

I join the queue, the dark-skinned, anxious, exhausted-looking queue of *extracomunitari* and wait, like all the others, patiently, part of the herd. A woman in front of me in the queue is giving the breast to her infant as she stands, naturally, unconcerned about her public nakedness, unconscious of the hungry looks of the men, the lewd comments. I step up to the counter where there is a sign saying *EXTRACOMUNITARI* in capital letters, and ask for *Ispettore* Lupo. I am told to wait. I sit down on the graffiti-covered bench against the wall and wait. Nothing happens. After an hour I rejoin the queue, and when my turn comes, repeat my request. Once again I am told, more impatiently this time, to wait. I return to the bench feeling heavy and tired and anxious.

The queue has grown shorter and at last straggles to an end. I return to the counter and struggle to catch the attention of one of the police clerks. He looks at me in irritation.

– *Che c'è ancora?* What is it this time?

I tell him I am waiting to see *Ispettore* Lupo.

– *È già andato via.* He's left. Come back on Monday.

As I walk back towards the bus stop my eyes catch sight of a small sign on an old building. *Pensione Arcadia.* I suddenly remember the receipt I found in my pocket yesterday. I look up at the building but there is nothing to be seen, just the brass plaque with the name and the single star beneath it.

I stand outside on the pavement, trying to understand. It disturbs me not to be able to remember. I know I have been here before, but it's a feeling on my skin like a ripple of recognition rather than a memory that I can locate. I try to push against the resistances of my mind a little, try to force the images to come. But it's like having a word on the tip of your tongue. I will have to wait for it to come of its own accord.

I wander on along the street. The plane trees are bare now, their trunks livid grey in the pale light of the street lamps. I remember reading somewhere that they will all have to be cut down soon, that they are hollowed out from within, diseased, their hearts dead. Their falling branches represent a danger to pedestrians and motorists.

Heavy traffic inches past, emitting clouds of exhaust fumes into the already polluted air. I am uncertain what to do. There are other people standing around like me and I realise that they are waiting for a bus. After a few minutes one arrives. I follow them on board and take a seat near the window. I watch the familiar streets pass by. I get off near Castel Sant'Angelo and walk down near the river, which glides past greasily after the October rains. Two canoes pass under the bridge near the far bank, the oarsmen rowing in unison, thin black shadows, their reflections repeating their shapes on the black waters.

It is dark as I walk back through the narrow streets towards the bus terminus. Under the deep porticoes figures emerge and retreat into the shadows. Women, mouths gaping in rage or laughter, pace to and fro in the cold night air. Their eyes meet mine, and then pass on, immediately excluding me as a client. An old man with a purple nose comes up to me, his tongue out, lips wet and covered in spittle, and rubs his fingers in my face, the age-old symbol of money, and I shake my head in confusion and turn away. Dark bird-shapes wing silently, just beyond vision, no more than a presence.

Cars sidle by, one stops. A woman steps up to the open window, takes in the details of the driver's lust. Sometimes this will be all he requires and he will speed away to spill his seed alone. Others, more literal, will invite her in and consummate their passion on the back seat of the car in the *piazzale* around the corner.

I pull my threadbare corduroy coat tighter around me, feeling the cold filter up into the sleeves and down the neck. I wrap my scarf up around my face so that only my eyes can be seen above the scratchy fabric. I feel conspicuous and try to pass by as quickly as I can. At last I see Sabrina. There is recognition, a half-smile, and the woman turns and leads the way towards a small hotel a block away. I follow.

Saturday 27 October
She is already gone when I awake in the morning, and I catch a bus down to the river. I walk across the ancient Roman bridge to Trastevere where I have discovered a second-hand bookseller who has a couple of stands, rather like steel *cassonetti,* that he locks at night but that open out into shelves full of strange books by day. I have started buying books by the box from him. Most of the time he has not even opened the boxes and has no idea what is in them – they are as they have arrived from the seller. Whatever is in them I read, as they have

been delivered to his stall. Often the owner of the books has died and his sons and daughters are getting rid of his earthly belongings as quickly as they can, getting rid of the things that formed the contours of his mind, that went to shape his thoughts and world. His children want nothing to do with that world, convinced that the world that they are creating around themselves will be infinitely superior and more interesting. Except that their children will do the same with their personal effects when the time comes. Sometimes, as I wander the streets I read the funeral announcements, black framed, on the walls or doors of the buildings, and I wonder if the books I am about to read belonged to this or that person. *Commendatore* Tommaso Cossuto, *Ingegner* Matteo Sbertoli, *Vedova* Elena Capecchi. I like to imagine their lives, governed by routine and social obligations, the little worries and concerns and niceties that occupied so many of their waking hours.

I buy a box of books from the bookseller and am curious to see what is inside, so I open it on the bus on my way back to Anzio. The books had evidently belonged to a certain *Avvocato* Mario Rossi. He had neatly written his name and the date into the front page of each book, in a rather old-fashioned flowing handwriting. I imagine a small, meticulous man. The books are all in immaculate condition, although they are obviously well read, with notes and passages underlined and bookmarks at favourite pages. There is a well-thumbed, clearly well-loved copy of the *Divina Commedia,* printed cheaply on furry pages that must have had to be cut open with a paper knife – the edges are still slightly frayed.

Amongst the books I discover a small cheaply printed one that looks particularly interesting to me. It is fragments of a *Diario,* written between 1554 and 1556 by a Florentine artist, Jacopo Carucci also known as Pontormo, after the name of the little town where he was born. I let it fall open by chance and my eyes stop on the following entries for a few days in the spring of 1556, just before he died, while he was busy painting the frescoes in the choir of San Lorenzo in Florence:

Tuesday evening I felt all weak and I ate a rosemary loaf and an omelette and salad and some dried figs.

Wednesday I fasted.

Thursday evening, omelette with one egg, a salad and four ounces of bread.

Friday evening, salad, pea soup and an omelette and five ounces of bread.

Saturday, butter, a rosemary bread, salad, sugar and an omelette.

Sunday 1st April I had lunch with Bronzino and I did not eat in the evening.

Monday evening I had steamed bread with butter, an omelette and two ounces of cake.

Tuesday

Wednesday

Thursday

Friday

On Saturday I went to the tavern; salad and omelette and cheese. I felt good.

This could be my diary.

It is very strange, to see him list these days that kept coming and departing with nothing to say for themselves. I think I would like to translate this book for myself.

Sunday 28 October

After lunch I walk up on the mountain, feeling a need to connect with my body, to draw my mind down into my body, this busy restless mind that leaves me so little rest. I set my foot to the little path that zigzags up through the bushes from behind the village. I pass the sign that says that the nesting season is now completed for the year and thanking me for not disturbing the birds – the sign has been there unchanged for the past three years. I walk upwards, feeling the tightening and release in my calf muscles, first one then the other, the rhythmic feel. I reach the first peak, my breath coming faster, recognising the beating of my heart in my chest, uncontrolled, or at least out of my control, my will. My mind is clearer now, focused on these physiological movements, on the dampness gathering in the hair at the nape of my neck. I wonder whether to take the contour, to limit the scope of my walk or to scale the highest peak. I decide that I need to extend myself, that I need to push through some kind of resistance, some barrier that is holding my thoughts, my emotions, in a limited frame, so I take the path that leads down into a little dell amidst a few last pine trees and then begins to climb, first to the shepherd's hut, then up the side of the buttress and on and up, climbing steeply so that I have to stop every few minutes to catch my breath, up to the radio mast, the highest point of the island. The sun is now high and I am sweating freely. I stop often to rest and drink water. I realise I am exhausted, that I have pushed beyond my own strength. I am thirsty, dehydrated, and have only a few sips of water left in my bottle. I wonder whether I should stop, go back, retrace my steps, but I figure that it will be shortest to go forward. I have been marching now for about three hours.

There are men working on the heavy cables that tie the radio mast to the earth; bound high up in the air they call from one to the other to check their progress, sharp bird-like cries high in the rarefied air. I wonder whether they can see me as I creep snail-like along the path at their feet. And then the descent, rapid, steep, lowering myself from rock to rock, afraid to twist my ankle, afraid to fall.

Monday 29 October
I am in my classroom when I see the ferry arrive. It is a windy grey day, the sea dark green and opaque with white spray rushing across the surface where the wind catches the tips of the waves. I sit correcting homework in between lessons, struggling to keep my mind focused on the simple thoughts of the children expressed in their even simpler words. Trying to pass time, which weighs heavily on me. I watch the little boats pull on their anchors, the old men sitting on the bench on the

jetty, talking, shouting garrulously at each other; even though
I can't hear their voices I know they are talking about politics
or sport or women. There is nothing else.

The ferry arrives in a mixture of engine fumes, the smell
of diesel oil and salt spray. I watch it manoeuvre and turn,
its rudder churning the green water white, as it backs into its
moorings. I watch the crew tie huge ropes to the bollards and
see the gangplank winched down, lowered from the stern. I
watch the passengers disembark, a handful of islanders; at this
time of the year there are no visitors. I see Ugo's uncle, holding
a little hand-pushed trolley, standing to one side waiting for the
fresh produce from the market to be unloaded. The seagulls
mewl and circle in the hope of scraps. I see a figure emerge, a
man dressed in a camel-hair coat with a hat low across his face.
A porter carries his suitcase to a waiting mini-taxi. He climbs
in next to the driver and the vehicle sets off up the hill.

For a few minutes my attention has been caught. I glance at
my watch. Twenty to two. I have lost ten minutes in all. I return
to the homework books. Fill the preposition into the sentence.
The exercises have been set especially to trap the children,
to make them think that the correct answer is the one that is
closest to the Italian form. None of them has noticed this – they
have all fallen into every trap. I shift my weight from one side to
the other, uncomfortable here on this hard wooden chair.

After school I go to the local grocer's to buy some eggs. I
stand and wait my turn. It takes about ten minutes before I am
served, and I know there will be a price to pay when I do at last
find myself face to face with the grocer. In exchange for what
I want to buy I will have to volunteer some small information
about myself, which will be passed on to the next customer
after I leave. But over the years I have grown quite adept at
avoiding questions that are too probing, that will give away
more than I am prepared to tell. And in any case the questions
asked will reflect the limits of the grocer's imagination so I am
not greatly at risk.

He greets me elaborately as if he hasn't seen me for months.

– *Buongiorno, e come sta la nostra signorina inglese?*

He is patronising as usual and exaggerates the pronunciation of the words. I return his greeting and tell him I want six eggs. He barely registers my order. That is going much too fast. First he wants to explore.

– *Ha visto che brutto tempo? Come a Londra, no? Si sentirà a casa sua. Piove sempre a Londra, non è vero?*

– Yes, I nod, it rains all the time in London. As if I knew.

Everyone shakes their heads in wonder at the madness of foreigners who live in such inhospitable places.

I decide to try a question of my own.

– Speaking of London, I saw a stranger arrive on the ferry this morning. Perhaps he is also from London?

At this everyone seems to have a comment but no one seems to know very much. It is true, there is a man and he is not from here. He is *un forestiero*, which could mean foreigner but could also just mean stranger; for the islanders the two concepts are indistinguishable. The taxi driver said that he had taken him to Villa Circe on the headland, which he has rented until the end of November. It appears that the man has come here to work. But to their intense frustration, he has managed to avoid further investigation. The taxi driver was paid at the door and no more information was forthcoming.

I admit that I also feel curious. Who could he be and what was he doing here, disturbing our simple retreat? Could he be German or English perhaps? The only other foreigner like me on the island. My eggs are at last wrapped, each individually in newspaper, and then placed carefully into a paper bag. I pay, greet everyone in the shop and leave.

I go home and make myself an omelette with two eggs and some cheese, then set out for a walk. Without even thinking about it I find myself walking up toward the headland. The wind is sharp and cold from the west and I feel my eyes and skin stinging as I struggle to hold to the path that runs along the top of the white shale cliffs. I see the turn-off to the house in the distance and I can see smoke rising from the chimney, but the house itself is hidden by vegetation and I can make out no other sign of life. I am not sure what I had been hoping for but I feel disappointed.

The clouds begin to clear as I make my way back home, and I walk along on to the jetty to watch the sunset. The water is clear and still in the chill autumn air, and I can see little fish, mullet probably, swimming back and forth under the wooden pilings. Their bodies flash and sparkle as they catch the sunlight filtered through the water, silver and blue as they turn in unison. I bend to look closer. Startled by my movement they seek refuge in the shadow of a beam, and then dance back into the light when they see there is no danger. Tenuous shivering of light in water.

It is late when I get home. Somehow, I'm not sure how, time has passed and it is 8.30. I will have to rush to get to Modugno's where I usually have supper. I still haven't corrected the homework books and I know that means that tomorrow I will have double the quantity to mark and won't have time for a walk. I feel dull and irritable. I pull on my jacket and walk quickly down the alley to the *trattoria*. From the street I recognise the slightly musty smell of the table linen, which has not been properly dried before being stored, the heavy bread that is only baked twice a week and which by Sunday is dry and crumbles easily when you break it.

Ugo's uncle is standing at the bar in the front room of the restaurant, red-faced, talking loudly and making lewd comments about the presenters on TV, strings of spittle forming between his thin lips. His eyes are bloodshot. As I walk through to the back room he orders another shot of grappa and tosses it back in one go, then slams the glass down on the counter with an exaggerated gesture. I wonder if it could be his voice that I hear sometimes at night, shouts echoing up the alley, a man's voice raised in anger, the sound of blows and then screaming, when I crouch at my window in the dark praying for it to stop. I pass through as quickly as I can to the dining room behind.

The stranger is here before me; he has taken my table.

I feel annoyed but find a place on the far side of the room. He gives no sign that he has noticed my resentment. Modugno waits on him attentively, hoping, I can see, that he will return as a regular during the dead season when trade is as thin as a stray dog. I strain to hear the man's accent when he places his order but he talks softly and I find it difficult to make out the words or distinguish the sounds. There is something slightly guttural about his voice although it sounds as if he is speaking English. Like me, he has brought a book to read.

I gaze with little interest at the hand-typed menu, noting yet again that the accent on the è is slightly off-centre. I suppose it is because it is used more than most of the other keys. I order soup and then cheese and salad. Modugno brings my meal, exchanges a few words with me, but his eyes are on the man, his words intended to create an impression on him rather than communicate with me, it is clear, and indeed it does not really bother me too much.

The lights are on along the harbour wall, the *lungomare*, when I come out of the restaurant, the coastguard vessel with *Finanza* printed in large white letters on the navy hull moored to one side. Seagulls, maddened by the bright spotlight on the end of the jetty, scream at the confusion of day with night. I walk down to the edge of the quay, feeling the sticky warm breeze from the desert lift my hair and skirt – it will rain in a few days, I know, but for now there is some respite from the cold of the winter that is closing in.

Old Cappi, the school secretary, is out and greets me. I nod in return and try to pass on. He touches my arm gently.

– *Come sta, Signorina? Che fa qui così tardi? Ha mangiato?*

Trying to relate. Trying to be kind. But I want none of it.

He is a widower and lives by himself in a tiny flat at the far end of the harbour. Every day he makes himself a plate of pasta for lunch with a glass of wine, and a *fettina* or ham and salad for supper. I know because he discusses it at the grocer's. I know what most people eat each day. I know most of what they do. There is no privacy here except in one's thoughts. All my movements, my habits, even my underwear is scrutinised as it hangs on the line stretched across the narrow alley from just below my window to the opposite building on a little pulley so that I can move the washing all the way across to catch the little sunlight that penetrates this far.

Tuesday 30 October
I have gone on reading Pontormo's *Diario* today. Strange how very plain and flat it is. I would have expected him to write about his visions and paintings. Yet all he talks about is the difficulty and daily discomfort of his life. I suppose that is what I keep doing too. The daily grind of survival that is so exhausting in its relentless monotony.

> Friday I got up an hour before dawn and I did that torso from the arm down.
> Saturday I did the thigh, and in the evening I cooked a piece of lamb.
> Today was Palm Sunday and I had lunch with Bronzino.
> Monday I did the head of that angel.
> Tuesday I stayed at home and I don't know what I did.
> Today was 1st April and I did the other thigh with the whole leg and foot.
> Holy Thursday.
> Friday I got up early and did the body of that child.

He eventually became a recluse, Pontormo that is, sealing himself, walling himself into the church of San Lorenzo in Florence, refusing to let anyone enter for over eleven years, and putting out a basket from the window for his supplies and communications with the outside world. Was he trying to keep out any form of change, trying to keep his existence totally under control? Here he painted scenes of the Creation and the Last Judgement, the Great Flood, scenes of heaven and hell.

Enough. My head is aching from all this reading and writing. The weather is warm today, unseasonably warm, the last breath of summer, so warm in fact that after school I pull on some shorts and a T-shirt. My legs and arms feel strange and white, exposed to the air after more than two months wrapped up in jackets and long pants. I pack a picnic lunch, some boiled eggs and a salad and bread, perhaps taking my cue from Pontormo, and some fruit and almonds and walnuts, and put them into my rucksack. It is still early when I set off up the hill. A slight warm breeze ripples the surface of the sea, and the sunlight sparkles and fragments off it. The shadows are longer and cooler than they would be in summer, but for the rest it feels like a June day, and within a short time I am sweating. I had planned to go to Chiaia di Luna to have a swim, but it is so hot that I begin to long for shade rather than the glare of the beach, so I head inland to the only natural source of water on the island, a small spring that is dry for most of the year but that is flowing after all the rain of the last month and has formed a deep pool in a grove of cork trees.

Strange brownish-green pebbles in running water, strange shapes, softly rounded, distorted by the lens of water. I dip my hand through the surface, seeing my skin turn greenish white, and the lines change strangely as my fingers reach down and touch the round stones on the bottom. I watch the fingers go from one to another as if they do not belong to my arm. They finally stop and choose one and lift it out. It is heavier than I expected as my hand comes into the air and reconnects to my body. The pebble is slippery with green slime. It smells slightly fishy. I feel a sense of sudden disgust. The play of light through the leaves and water on to the pebbles has been lost and all that is left is this smelly slimy stone. I dip my hand in again.

A bird call rouses me from my thoughts. I breathe deeply and look up at the branches, wondering where the song came from. I open my bag and bring out the picnic I had prepared in my apartment hours ago, the hard-boiled eggs, the cheese, the salad, the buttered bread – a little feast. I have never got used to the local habit of eating unbuttered bread. I lay it out on a little tablecloth I had folded into a corner of the bag, then look at it listlessly. I don't feel hungry. I return to the little stream. It barely deserves the name, just a trickle of water really, but it feeds this pool that is full of frogs and tadpoles and salamanders. The frogs, now that they are used to my presence and are no longer afraid of the shadow I cast across the water where before there had only been dancing light, croak noisily to each other from the shallows. I watch for some time, mesmerised by the flitting light and shadow on the water, and then eventually grow bored. I turn back to the picnic laid out on the bank, but it still looks uninteresting. I lie back on the soft loamy earth and close my eyes.

A picture forms in my mind of the park where we used to play as children, the scent of summer and growth, full of big trees and secret places and a pond covered with lotus flowers. But swirling beneath the surface the pond was treacherous, deep with unknown currents.

My mother used to warn me: 'Don't go near the water, you might slip and the current will pull you down!'

I remember wondering what a current was. And suddenly I knew. It was a giant octopus with long tentacles that would grab me and pull me down, down, into the deep darkness. No air, no breath, no life, just a cold watery grave, with my hair and eyes and mouth and throat and stomach all awash.

I picture myself lying there on the grass some distance from the pond, a small child in shorts and a T-shirt. When I go there with my brothers, I no longer play with them. I just lie there and watch it. I am sure that if I watch carefully enough, sooner or later I will see the current, catch a flash of a tentacle. From time to time the water ripples as if something were moving in the depths. But then it passes and the pond settles and the sun shines on the undisturbed surface again.

It is late afternoon when I awake. The shadows are long and my body is stiff and cold. I pull myself awkwardly to my feet, brush the leaves off my clothes and pack away my lunch untouched. I know I have been dreaming deeply but can't quite remember the images that hang tantalisingly just out of consciousness, just out of sight. I put my rucksack over one shoulder and begin the long walk back to the village, anxious to get home before it is completely dark.

Wednesday 31 October

Today I am caught up in midterm tests and marking and teachers' meetings, which I resent but can do nothing about. I am forced to attend. I sit as far back as possible and try to avoid the gossip and idle conversations with the other members of staff. It is not too hard. They don't consider me one of themselves, both because I am a temporary teacher and because I am not Italian. One of the teachers is trying to persuade me to approach the unions about my precarious position here. She says that it is illegal for them to employ me on a temporary basis for so long and then possibly even send me away, that after a certain amount of time by law my status should become permanent. I do not feel like challenging the Italian government on a matter about which I feel so little enthusiasm or entitlement, but I don't even have enough energy to explain this to her so I am forced to hear her out. My attention flickers backwards and forwards between the voices in the room and my memory of the pool, the sparkling light on the little fish.

I found my umbrella today, behind the classroom door where I must have left it last year, or perhaps the year before. It was covered in dust and the joints were stiff and slightly rusty, the fabric hardened and brittle, but it opened up after a few attempts. I will not need to buy a new one after all. It is beginning to look like rain again so I feel quite pleased to have it.

As I am leaving the school at lunchtime Signor Cappi calls me into the office to tell me that I am wanted on the phone. I lift the receiver.

– *Pronto?*

– *Perchè non è venuta venerdì?* He doesn't give his name but I recognise the hollow dry voice at once. It is *Ispettore* Lupo again.

I hesitate.

– *Deve ritornare. L'aspetto questo venerdì.* I will expect you on Friday. Don't forget. Make sure you come this time.

He puts down the phone. I haven't said a word.

I hurry out under my umbrella feeling upset. I notice that Ugo is hovering outside the school gate. It crosses my mind that he is waiting for me. Perhaps he wants me to protect him against the other boys, now that I have saved him once. I pass through, ignoring him. I walk home quickly and close and lock the door behind me. I feel agitated. I suspect that he is following me but I know I have to keep him out. I have no place for him in my life.

Thursday 1 November

Today is the first of November, All Saints' Day. *I Morti.* Feast of the Dead. Every year families prepare picnics of cold pasta and roast meats and vegetables and hard biscuits called *ossa dei morti*, bones of the dead, and spend the day at the cemetery, old people, parents, children, connecting the dead with the living. The day is festive, everyone dressed in their best, chatting with friends and relatives from distant parts of the island on the edge of the grave. There is a greater familiarity with death here than where I come from. Children grow up aware of those who have lived here before them, knowing that at some point they too will lie here in this consecrated ground while their descendants laugh and talk above their bodies. Yet even here things are changing, and people leave the island and never come back and their bones are cremated and the ashes dispersed in places that do not know the weight of their tread.

There is no school because of the holiday. I set off early for a long walk, and then return to my little apartment. I know I have a pile of marking to do but I feel strangely restless and unable to settle down to anything. I sit at my window and try to read but I find myself reading the same sentence over and over again without being able to make any sense of it at all. I try to translate a few lines of Pontormo's *Diario*.

Sunday and Monday I cooked myself a bit of veal that Bastiano bought for me and I spent the two days at home drawing and I had dinner by myself those three days.

Tuesday 29th October

Wednesday 30.

At last I put down my book and just stare out of the window at the rooftops and the grey sea beyond. My thoughts flit aimlessly here and there, often returning to the same place and sparking the same reaction, then moving on like a butterfly, an insect. I think of work, of Ugo, of Leonardo and Matteo, of *Ispettore* Lupo, and I feel a sense of growing unease in my stomach. Tomorrow is Friday and I will have to go and see him. What is it he wants from me? What does he know about me? Then I think of dinner and what I will have to eat at Modugno's. And then back to Ugo and Leonardo.

Friday 2 November

Rain has closed in over the little village again today. I can't remember such a grey rainy November in all my years here. I hear that there have been floods all over Italy, that the Po has broken its banks and many farms have been isolated. The water just keeps coming down. It is difficult to distinguish the sea from the sky when I look out, all just a grey union.

It is Friday and I know I must go and see *Ispettore* Lupo. After school I quickly prepare an overnight bag and rush down to the harbour to catch the ferry. I feel pleased to get away from the children and the island. I can hear the older boys' voices echoing through the village streets, singing a scurrilous song in mock Gregorian chant:

> *Qui si celebra il mistero di San Cirillo*
> *che con il cazzo fatto a spillo*
> *inculava i microbi.*

They draw it out long on the final note, and then burst into mocking laughter. I try to translate the words in my head but as usual English doesn't quite catch the sexual nuances. The word *prick* is so prim. I will first go and see *Ispettore* Lupo and then maybe catch a train to Florence to see the *Deposition from the Cross* by Pontormo in the Santa Felicità church.

In his *Diario* there are some sketches that he did for the Choir of San Lorenzo, which are all that remained after the frescoes were destroyed in 1742. I find them fascinating, these massed bodies, twisted, intertwined, of the dead on the day of the Last Judgement, of bodies entangled, limbs disembodied, parts that do not belong anywhere, arms that appear from under someone else's chest. When he painted he often used blue. Blue-tinged flesh, blue like the sky, the blue of lapis lazuli which he ground and mixed into his paint. But these sketches are earth coloured, *terra cotta*, burnt earth.

I take a seat on the upper level of the ferry since all the seats below are occupied. I rub the window with my sleeve to clear the mist and see a taxi stop on the dock, and the stranger emerge. I can't see his face, which is obscured by the large black umbrella he holds to protect himself from the rain. He disappears from my sight as he enters the wide-open maw of the ferry, then he reappears at the entrance to the lounge. He sits in the only free seat a few rows ahead of me. I try to focus on my book, my rough translation of the *Diario:*

> On Tuesday I had half a kid's head and soup for dinner.
> Wednesday I had the other half and some sweet wine and five
> ounces of bread and a caper salad.
> Thursday evening a hearty beef soup and salad.

Pontormo carries on and on about the minute details of his life, of what he ate, of his bowel movements, as if these were the most important things, the ones he felt it was important to record for his own understanding, for posterity:

> On Tuesday evening I ate a green salad and an omelette.

On Ash Wednesday two farthings of almonds and an omelette and walnuts and I worked on that figure above the skull (figure).

Thursday evening a green salad and caviar and an egg; the Duchess came to San Lorenzo and the Duke accompanied her.

Friday evening an omelette, some broad beans and a bit of caviar and four ounces of bread.

Saturday evening I ate two eggs.

Sunday, which was Easter Sunday, I went to lunch with Bronzino and I had dinner with him too.

It is getting dark by the time the ferry arrives in Anzio. In the bustle at the harbour I lose sight of the man. I catch the bus through to Rome and wander along the rainy streets, the mulch of wet fallen leaves clinging to my shoes. By late afternoon I am in front of the *Questura* again. Nothing seems to have changed from my last visit. Even the faces look the same. I wait in the same tired queue, recognising the particular depressed smell of this place from the last time, a smell of nervous perspiration and poverty. I feel myself falling into a state of helpless lethargy like everyone else. After about an hour my turn comes. I ask for *Ispettore* Lupo. I am directed to a side corridor, second floor, and third door to the left. I wait for the lift with an elderly peasant woman who looks frightened as the door slides open. She turns away in confusion.

– *Mi si schianta il core.* My heart is going to burst, she mutters to herself cryptically.

I wander along the poorly lit corridor and at last come to the door. I knock and enter.

He is sitting at a desk writing in a large ledger: a pale man with pale eyes, wearing the grey-blue trousers of the police with a crimson stripe down the side of the leg. He takes no notice of me when I enter, but I know he is aware of my presence because the pen stops moving, hangs suspended for a second in mid-air, and then his pale fingers, bluish around the nails, brush a scrap of dust off the page.

– *Permesso*? I say.

He coughs but doesn't reply. I walk up to the desk anyway. The room smells of stale smoke.

– *Ispettore* Lupo? I ask.

– *Si. Mi dica,* he says at last without lifting his head from his ledger.

– You wanted to talk to me? You called. You asked me to come. My name is Anna P.

His eyes lift slowly off the ledger, flicker over my face, appear for a moment to be looking for something he can't quite locate, and then suddenly, almost violently, latch on to my eyes. I pull back with a jerk. He smiles.

– *Ah, la Signorina P.*

He examines me carefully.

– *Finalmente. Era ora.*

He opens one of the drawers in the desk and pulls out a small bundle of files. I notice a half-empty bottle of brandy lying next to them in the drawer. He notices my glance and quickly pushes the drawer shut. He sits back in his chair and slowly raises his pale eyes again to meet mine. He stares at me impassively.

– *Perchè non si è presentata prima?*

That accusing tone again. I am not sure what to say. He drops his eyes to the file and pages through document after document and at last finds what he was looking for.

– *Mi dìa il passaporto.*

I hand him my passport. He takes it, looks at the photograph, and then gets up and leaves the room without saying a word. I wait standing in front of the desk for a few minutes and finally sit down on the edge of the bench beneath the high barred window. Half an hour passes. I go to the door at last but the corridor is empty so I sit down again and wait for another quarter of an hour. Eventually I hear his dry cough in the passage and he reappears at the door. He does not excuse himself for his absence but sits down and stares at me again.

– *Allora, mi dica.* So, what do you want?

I look at him in surprise.

– What do *you* want? You asked me to come.

He takes a packet of cigarettes out of his pocket, puts one between his lips, strikes a match and lights it. The glow from the flame lights up the hollows of his face, emphasising his gauntness. He inhales deeply.

– *Lo sa perchè è qui, vero?* You know why you're here, don't you?

He speaks slowly in a thin dry voice. Is he just a bully, I wonder, or does he know something about me that I don't know?

I shake my head, no.

– *Ma sì che lo sa.* Yes, of course you know.

He smiles, a cold, unamused smile.

– *Le autorità chiedono notizie di Lei. Ci sono delle irregolarità.* Questions are being asked about you. People upstairs want to know more. They want information.

He gestures upward with his chin.

I feel myself spinning, falling into confusion.

– Questions?

He smiles.

As if we were just chatting, chance acquaintances on a train, he asks:

– *Da quanto tempo è in Italia?* How long have you been in Italy?

I stare out of the barred window at the darkening sky. A bird flies past heavily.

– *Perchè è venuta qui? Perchè ha lasciato il Sudafrica?* Why did you leave South Africa?

I don't reply. He pauses for a minute and then continues, irritated.

– *Non mi risponde. Ma che, è muta Lei?* Why don't you answer me? Are you mute or something?

I breathe deeply.

– *E poi, abbiamo controllato la sua pratica. Mancano dei documenti.* You had better know something. We've checked your records – there are documents missing.

He points at the file.

There is a sinking feeling in my stomach.

– What is missing?

– *Ma come, non lo sa*? Don't you know?

I shrug.

– *Manca il certificato di nascita per comminciare.* Your birth certificate is missing. *Perchè manca*? Why is it missing?

I look at him in surprise. I had been expecting much worse than that. They must have my birth certificate. It was part of my application years ago. They must have lost or mislaid it.

– What is it that you want from me?

He looks at me again with cold eyes.

– We are going to apply to the South African authorities for this document. While we are about it we will also ask for a *Nulla Osta,* for your police record. Just in case. I think it will not take long. You must come back so that we can talk. *Capisce*?

I shrug.

– *Stia attenta, Signorina.* Be careful. Things are not what they seem.

He looks at me intently.

Flame tugs at the edges, at the dark whorls of my mind.

There is a knock on the door. A uniformed policeman steps into the room and salutes.

– *La vogliono di sopra.*

Lupo grunts, nods and rises. He looks at me.

– I am wanted upstairs. *Ora può andare.* You may go. But we need to talk further. *Torni ancora a vedermi. Venerdì prossimo.* Next Friday. *Le va bene*?

I open my mouth to object, but he interrupts at once.

– *Dobbiamo parlare ancora.* There are other matters. *Capisce*? Come again next Friday.

It is not a question. I nod, feeling trapped.

He shows me to the door and disappears down the corridor. It suddenly occurs to me that he has not returned my passport.

I make my way back to the main hall, but the queue is now gone and there is no one about. I go to the entrance. There is a policeman on duty there. I try to explain what has happened, that my passport has been taken, but his task is simply to keep the entrance clear and he pushes me rudely away and outside. When I try to come back inside he tells me that the offices are now closed and that I should come back on Monday.

I wander through the streets uncertain what to do or where to go. I am reluctant to go back to the island without my passport, but I haven't brought my identity card with me and I can't stay overnight in a hotel without a document. I stop at a *caffè* and order a coffee, which I drink standing up, then walk on. It is dark already, cold and drizzling, and workers are rushing from their offices to the comfort of their homes, to a warm meal and to an evening spent dozing in front of the television. I can feel the damp penetrating through the fabric of my worn coat.

I wander aimlessly towards the centre of town getting more and more lost in the maze of tiny streets and alleys. None of them runs straight so I have no idea after a while what direction I am going in. I have no idea where I am, nor does it seem very important to know. My feet are growing sore and tired so I go into the bar next to the station, which stays open all night. I push open the door, wipe my feet in the sawdust spread across the entrance, and enter.

It is dimly lit. A jukebox is playing hits from the seventies in the corner, something by Orietta Berti and Massimo Ranieri, competing with the voices on the TV. Two or three men slouch in white plastic chairs watching TV on a screen suspended from the ceiling. The tired-looking barman idly polishes a glass with a stained cloth. I don't normally drink spirits but I am cold and suddenly very weary and weak, so I order a *caffè corretto* with brandy. I pay and carry it over to a little table in the corner where I sit down and unbutton my coat. The TV is showing Formula One racing, the cars whining like insects as they pass the camera. One of the men starts talking, a rambling story full of invectives against the government, which in his opinion is squandering taxpayers' money. He describes it all as a *Pozzo di San Patrizio*, a bottomless well that they keep dipping into. He falls silent for a while and then orders another glass of wine. He drinks it in a single gulp and points with his finger to show that he wants it refilled. He begins to speak again to no one in particular and indeed no one seems to be listening, except me, but I have my eyes closed and am pretending not to, or perhaps the barman who is maybe listening more to the man's tone of voice than the words. He speaks of prison, of how he always commits a small crime and allows himself to be caught just before the winter really starts, so that he will have a roof over his head for the very cold months. The problem is how to calibrate the offence so that he will be given a sentence long enough to last the winter but that will set him free once the sap starts to rise in his veins again in springtime. He goes on and on about people he has met inside, about a woman he knows outside. My eyes grow heavy and my head aches. I order another coffee with brandy, but it just makes my stomach burn and I push it to one side at last. I look at my watch. It is already 4 am. Too late to do anything else. I will just have to stay until morning or until they close. It is as good a plan as any, and at least it is dry. I lean my head against the wall and close my eyes. The background noise continues lulling me into sleep. From time to time I wake up and become conscious that my mouth is open, my posture sagging, and I straighten myself and try to bring order to my disordered thoughts until sleep overcomes me once more. I half wake at one point and find that the man is sitting by my side, his arm around my shoulders, but I can't rouse myself and at last I fall into a fitful sleep, full of disturbing dreams. Black birds tumble, roll, slide, heave, a shapeless mass of unformed, seething life, the primordial confusion of life and death, of body parts fragmenting, decomposing and recomposing. A policeman sits in the shadows and laughs and offers me a platter with a bloodied head on it. I try to escape, I try to run but my legs are trapped in the black decomposing matter. My dreams are interspersed with moments of uncomfortable wakefulness in which I become aware of my stale mouth, my damp clothes, of unknown hands touching my body, of my discomfort at sleeping on a hard chair.

Saturday 3 November

At six o'clock I stand up and go to the bathroom. I tidy myself as best I can in the tiny bathroom stacked high with empty beer crates, then go next door to the bus terminus.

I catch the first bus to Anzio, but traffic is heavy and the ferry has already left when we arrive. I check the timetable on the board. The next one leaves at 10 am. I will have to wait for three hours. No *caffè*s or restaurants are open at this time of the morning out of season, so I huddle on a bench outside the ticket office. It is cold and damp in my thin coat and the hours pass slowly. I get up from time to time to stamp my feet when they grow numb. My mind keeps going back to Lupo's question – why are you here? How long have you been here? What are you doing here in Italy? Why did you leave South Africa? I try to work it out but I have no explanation. Such confusion in my mind.

Sunday 4 November

Monday 5 November

There are many deaths at this time of the year. The children came across a dead sparrow in the playground this morning, fallen from its branch in the chill of midnight. I touched it with the toe of my shoe but it was stiff and cold.

Tuesday 6 November

After school I see Matteo and Leonardo standing at the *edicola* gazing intently at the pornographic magazines on display, until the newsagent shouts at them to go away.

Wednesday 7 November

Dinner at Modugno's. It feels more dingy than usual tonight. I order pasta and wine. Out of habit I pull out my book and prop it up in front of me on the table. My mind is again caught by Pontormo:

> On Tuesday the weather was fine and in the evening I dined on 10 ounces of bread.
> Wednesday morning it was cold and I stayed at home; I dined on 9 ounces of bread and the finest lamb.
> Thursday I worked on those two arms and I dined on 9 ounces of bread, meat and cheese and it was quite cold.
> Friday I did the head with that rock beneath it. I ate 9 ounces of bread, an omelette and salad and my head felt dizzy.
> Saturday I did the chest and the hand and I dined on 10 ounces of bread.
> On Sunday I ate 10 ounces of bread and I spent all day feeling weak and tired and irritable – the weather was beautiful and it was full moon.
> Monday 22nd April I felt well – all my complaints had vanished – I ate 8 ounces of bread. I wasn't dizzy and I wasn't weak and I felt hopeful.

Thursday 8 November

After school I walk up to the headland. The house looks abandoned. On an impulse I take the track to the left that leads past it to the beach. The track is overgrown with grasses and aromatic plants that release strong smells as I brush against them. I follow it until I reach a narrow path that zigzags down to the beach far below. There are no handrails and the path is badly eroded. I make way down it cautiously, climbing over boulders and rocks and afraid to fall.

I take off my shoes and walk from one end of the beach to the other, then lie down on the black volcanic sand and gaze up at the sky. Soft flopping of little waves at the water's edge. Dark clouds hang on the horizon. Seagulls soar high overhead.

I stretch my arms wide in imitation of their flight, and my fingers encounter something hard buried in the sand. I turn to look. Bird bones bleached white by salt and light. Skeleton of a tiny bird, huge sockets where once were eyes. Tiny brain contained: a life, a world enclosed in bone. I rub it between my fingers into fragments, grains of white on black.

I see the figure of a man silhouetted against the cliff top. He doesn't seem to have noticed me. He stands for a few minutes gazing out to sea. I turn to see if I can make out what it is he is looking at. When I turn again he is gone.

Friday 9 November
It is Friday today and I must go and see *Ispettore* Lupo again. The small *aliscafo* takes just over an hour for the crossing.

It is strange how little I remember of these journeys. Often it is only as I disembark again on the island after the weekend that I suddenly become aware of what is going on. Of course no one here knows what I do when I go to the mainland, and even I find it difficult to remember the time I spend there. It's as if it were shrouded in mist, the sea passage forming a boundary between worlds. Here on the island everything is normal, controllable, measured, my emotions muted, my existence repetitive. Across the straits it is all out of my control.

By four o'clock I am outside the *Questura*. It looks dirtier and more depressing than ever. This time I don't wait in the queue, but go directly along the passage to *Ispettore* Lupo's office. The door is ajar. He is standing at his desk talking to another policeman. He sees me at the door and waves me in. He seems amused at something, a private joke between them.

– *La Signorina P! Eccola. Ben tornata. L'aspettavo da tempo. Si accomodi.*

I sit on the only chair available, a cheap plastic chair. He looks knowingly at his colleague, then opens his drawer and pulls out the same bundle of files as the last time.

– I have only come to fetch my passport. You have no right to keep it.

– *Si, ma non abbiamo finito la nostra conversazione, vero.*

– I still don't know what you want from me. I have nothing to tell you. I have come all the way from Ponza to see you and get my passport. Please give it to me and let me go home.

– *Certo. Ma prima dobbiamo parlare.*

He looks at me again. There is something different in his expression now, something has shifted. His eyes flicker downwards over my body, examine me briefly, and then rise to meet mine. I feel my stomach contract.

– *Dov'era il 2 Novembre?*

– I beg your pardon? What did you say?

– *Il 2 Novembre. Dov'era.* Where were you?

– I don't know where I was on the second. Probably at school on the island.

– *Mi sa che racconta bugie.* I think you're lying. I think you do know. And what can you tell me about the *Pensione Arcadia?*

I feel myself go cold.

– Why do you ask me that?

– What do you know about it?

– I may have seen it in passing. I may even have stayed there. So what?

He pulls a photograph out of the folder and shows it to me. In it I see a city street with a car, a mustard-coloured Cinquecento parked in front of a building. There is a sign on the wall behind it. *Pensione Arcadia.* He looks at me intently.

– *Ma è proprio sicura?* Are you sure that's all?

Again I don't reply.

He picks up a piece of paper.

– *Ci risulta che Lei ha affittato una stanza per qualche ora in un albergo di questo nome vicino alla Stazione Termini. Ora si riccorda? Il 2 Novembre.* You rented a room at the *Pensione Arcadia* near the station on the second of November. Your name was in the register.

– I don't remember, but what if I did? What is it to you? Where are you trying to go with this?

– *Stia attenta, Signorina. Mi risponda con cura, mi raccomando.* Be careful what you say. Answer carefully, I'm warning you.

– Perhaps I was there. I don't remember. I sometimes spend the night in Rome and take a room in a *pensione*. I don't always take note of the name. I just go to the first one I find.

– *Ma è proprio sicura? Ci ha pensato bene?* Are you sure? Have you thought about this properly?

– Why do you want to know?

– A man died there that night. The hotel manager. His body was found on the stairs the next morning. *Era morto.* We suspect it was not an accident. We are making contact with everyone who spent the night in the *pensione. E allora mi dica,* did you see or hear anything?

– No.

– You mean you remember being there but no, you didn't hear anything?

– No, I don't remember anything.

And it is true. I don't remember anything. I feel a sense of panic rise in me. If my name was in the register I must have been there. But I have no memory of it. And if I don't, who did spend the night there? But I don't want this policeman investigating. I feel deeply disturbed by the conversation. What does he know about me?

We continue for a few more minutes, then he tells me I can leave. He tells me to return next Friday after we have both given the matter some thought. He tells me not to leave Italy until I have spoken to him again. I think he is just trying to scare me but I don't really know. He still hasn't returned my passport.

I go out into the street and sit down in a bar and order a cup of tea. My thoughts are swirling. I don't remember the *Pensione Arcadia* even though I know now for sure that I have been there. But the mustard-coloured Cinquecento? I do remember that. But there are no images attached. Strange flat emotionless memories.

I don't know where to go or what to do. I know I can't go and look for Sabrina since the police are probably watching out for me. I finally resolve that what I need is movement away, and that I will catch the first train out of the station, wherever it is going. I will let fate decide.

The first train, coming from Palermo, is arriving in twenty minutes and heading north to Frankfurt, passing through Florence on its way. That confirms it. I am going to Florence to see the *Deposition* by Pontormo after all. I wait on the platform with two or three other travellers, watching the track to where it curves out of sight amongst a sprawl of apartment blocks and TV aerials. It is still light but the darkness of evening is just beginning to creep in from the east. The train, shiny with rain, limps slowly into the station. I follow the general movement. I climb the stairs to the door and step into the corridor. It is packed full of people sitting everywhere, in the compartments, on suitcases in the passage, pressed against the steamed-up windows. I push my way through the mass of bodies and by luck find a seat in one of the compartments. The air is heavy and stale. Clearly the other passengers have spent all day travelling. Some are asleep, their bodies abandoned against the green plastic seats.

I sit in the train and slip into a half sleep. It is warm and comfortable and my breathing deepens. I catch hold of myself, force my eyes back open, glance at the man sitting next to me, check my watch, twenty minutes to go to the next station. I see him glance sideways, his eyes on my thighs in the skirt and dark stockings. I adjust my position slightly, re-cross my legs, feeling my skirt hitch up slightly but not prepared to do anything about it. I feel too drowsy, the compartment too warm. I am flushed, aware of my body scent, lulled by the gentle swaying of the high-speed train. I force myself awake again, look out of the window at the fallow fields that have been ploughed in readiness for spring, the greasy soil of the Tiber valley, which the plough has turned slowly, slicing and turning it into furrows over and over across the wide plain.

Low grey clouds hang heavy overhead, promising more rain.

The outskirts of a town flash past, confused and ugly, and now the landscape is changing, the hills are rising up on the left of the train, bringing embankments covered in shrubs and mimosas into view, while the land drops away invisible on the other. The train slows as it enters a tunnel, and the compartment darkens, then lightens again as we come through. I feel the man move beside me in his seat, his thigh grazes mine, then he is still, our legs touching. I close my eyes, uncertain, then let go, relinquish control. Wait to see what will happen. Vaguely curious, more sleepy than anything else. Comfortable, warm, the pressure from his thigh increases, now it is not just by accident, no longer casual, it is deliberate, there is intention in it. If I want it to stop, now is the moment. I breathe deeply and don't move. The train enters another tunnel and the compartment falls into complete darkness. I feel his hand touch my knee, hesitate for a moment then begin to rise. I allow my legs to fall slack, open, feel his hand slipping between them and up, touching, aware now that there is no barrier, the fingers probe, penetrate deeply, then withdraw and the train trundles out again into the daylight. The other passengers have noticed nothing but I draw myself up on my seat and cross my legs. He is looking out of the far window as if completely unaware, *ignaro*, of my presence, his hands folded loosely in his lap. A few minutes later we reach our destination and the train pulls into the station. I feel him brush against me from behind as we push our way along the narrow passageway to the door. I feel his presence behind me again as I stand at the top of the steps looking out at the platform; I pause for a moment, then step down off the train and lose him in the crowd.

I walk towards the river and then turn left and follow the Lungarno Corsini upstream, listening to the soft accents of the people, the aspirated Etruscan sounds that so characterise the local speech. I cross over at the Ponte Vecchio to the little church of Santa Felicità, one of the oldest in Florence. The church is dark and empty. The high nave and pillars running along the main body of the church make it feel austere and spiritual, different from the theatrical overabundance, the false marble and papier mâché mouldings of the baroque churches further south. The painting I am seeking is in a little chapel to the right. There is a high wrought-iron grating across the front of the chapel, which impedes access to the *Deposition*. You can look through the bars but go no closer.

I put some coins into a slot and the lights come on and illuminate what I have come to see: Pontormo's *Deposition*. The Madonna gazes longingly towards her dead son, while the helpers lift his heavy inert body from the cross. It is a strange scene full of grief and sorrow and yearning, almost suspended in air. The figures bearing the weight of the body barely touch the ground, as if in a sense they were dancing. The centre of the painting is empty – all the figures are around the sides, including the lifeless body of Christ, which is draped across the bottom. The bodies entwine and merge into a knot so that it is almost impossible to work out which limb belongs to whom, but it is clear that there is one arm too many. The flesh has a bluish tinge to it.

I sit on a hard wooden pew and gaze up at the scene. It makes me uncomfortable not to know where that arm belongs. I know I should be able to work it out but my mind feels as if it is slipping and I can't quite keep my focus. My head is bursting, throbbing from lack of sleep. The light goes out and I am left sitting alone in the dark. An old woman, thin, grey-faced, silently enters the church and crosses herself. She kneels next to me in front of the *Deposition*, prays for a few seconds and then settles back on to the pew waiting to be confessed. A priest shuffles into the church from a side door, takes his seat in the dark wooden confessional box tucked against a pillar and closes the curtain behind him. At a signal that I do not catch, the woman gets up, goes to kneel at the side of the box and begins to whisper through the wooden grate.

The words are indistinct but the whispering fills the chapel and echoes up through the vault. The woman's voice disturbs me, a keening that goes on and on, interspersed from time to time by the deeper reassuring voice of the priest. It feels as if the pain will never stop. After a while I get up and light a single candle with a match from the box that is tied with a piece of dirty string to the leg of the table on which stand rows and rows of burnt-out stumps, offerings by the faithful that no one has bothered to clean away. I watch the candlelight flicker over the surface of the fresco, picking up the grain. I wish I could pray but I would not know what to pray for, nor how to do it. I kneel and fold my hands in front of me as I was taught to do as a small child at bedtime but the thoughts and words will not come. I can not imagine myself talking to anyone.

At last I sit back on the seat feeling my knees sore and stiff. I get up to go, then feel reluctant to leave this place. I put out some more money and take two more candles. I place them carefully in the little metal clasps in line with the first one and light them, watching the flame catch alight and begin to glow warmly with a golden self-contained life. I stand and watch entranced the three little flames in the high cold dark church. The woman leaves the confessional and kneels again in the darkened pew and I turn my back and come out into the daylight and get caught up in the hordes of tourists pushing their way across the bridge. So many people. I try to imagine what it must have been like at Pontormo's time. The same buildings stand as they did then; he too must have crossed the Ponte Vecchio to reach the church from where he lived each day. There was bad damage to the city during the war, and all the other bridges were blown up, but this bridge was never touched even though the Germans were aware that the Partisans were using the secret corridor to move backwards and forwards across the river.

I turn into the side streets to avoid the crowds, and catch a glimpse of myself reflected in a shop window, distorted, swollen, with dark eyes. I look away quickly, not liking what I see.

My eyes are inexplicably drawn to a shop across the street. I cross and look into the window. It is a *casalinghi*, a shop that sells household goods. The display is set up for a wedding register even though this is not the season for weddings: fine porcelains, silverware, *bomboniere*, pots and pans, a row of knives. A thought insinuates itself into my brain and will not shift, it sticks there like some primordial underwater sucking thing.

I enter the shop. A little bell rings as I step over the threshold, and an elderly woman steps out of a back room to serve me. She stubs out a cigarette in a metal ashtray next to the till.

– I would like a knife, I say. I need a knife.

Her eyes run impassively over my face.

– *Che tipo di coltello?*

– Like the one in the window. I point.

She coughs, a rasping, spitting sound, and pulls aside the little curtain that acts as the backdrop to the display in the window and extracts the tray with the knives.

– *Quale vuole?*

I stretch out my hand to pick up the knife, but she quickly pulls the tray away.

– *Non si tocca.* You may not touch it.

– That one, I say, pointing.

She grunts in assent, then picks it up and holds it against her hand, moving it from side to side. It sparkles in the light that penetrates from the window.

– How much is it? I gesture towards the knife.

She names the price, doubled I am sure because of what she perceives is an English accent, the illusion of foreign wealth. I accept and draw out the money. She wraps the knife carefully first in tissue paper, then in wedding gift wrap, white with silver wedding bells and the words *Tanti Auguri,* Congratulations, repeated over and over. The transaction is done. The little bell rings behind me as I step back out into the street. Dark birds wheel in the sky, a black ball of them that turns as one, becoming silver as it reflects the rays of the setting sun, then black again as it turns away. Then suddenly the ball shatters and the birds fly off in all directions like dark thoughts across the sky.

I feel reluctant to go back to the station when I leave the shop, so I wander back down towards the river. It is late afternoon by now and the shadows are long. Birds are gathering in holes in buildings, under bridges, wherever they can find a place, a little protection, for all creatures seek protection from the elements when dark falls, except for those that hunt by night. I stand on the embankment gazing out across the ancient stream, polluted now after so many centuries' contact with man. There is someone standing a few metres from me, also intent on looking out, but I can't make out his features in the dark.

Today Sunday 7th January 1554 I fell and sprained my shoulder and arm. I was in pain so I spent six days at Bronzino's house, then I returned home and was ill until Carnival which was on the 6th February 1554.

Sunday morning the 11th March 1554 I went to lunch with Bronzino, chicken and veal, and I felt well (so much so that when they came to fetch me at home I was in bed – it was quite late and when I got up I felt swollen and full – it was quite a good day). In the evening I had some roast salt beef that made me thirsty and on Monday evening I dined on cabbage and an omelette.

I walk heavily back to the station, along narrow streets, dodging cars parked on the pavement and huge rubbish bins overflowing with garbage. The discarded parts of our lives. People finding sources of sustenance even here. Food only partly spoiled. Shoes not totally worn through, a broken chair, a mouldy mattress that will still protect you from the frozen earth. Little things that matter when all else is lost. When a thin rag to cover the ground is all that is left between you and the grave.

I catch the first train south and by the evening I am back in my apartment. My little bird's water bowl is completely dry and it looks frightened and distressed. I try to talk to it and put my finger through the bars for it to peck but it huddles in a corner and stares at me with scared eyes so I put the cover over the cage and go to bed.

Sunday 11 November
I mark homework all morning.

Monday 12 November
Leonardo has not done his homework, or so he says, although I am certain that his mother would have checked and insisted that he should do it. There is an edge of pride to his statement and he stares at me defiantly when I ask for his book. I am not sure what to do. If I make an incident of it I will be playing into his hands, yet I can't ignore it either.

– You'll have to do it for tomorrow then, and bring a note from your mother.

– *Ma maestra, ci'ho tanti compiti per domani. Non posso.*

– I don't care how much homework you have for tomorrow, you will have it here on my desk by nine o'clock. Do you understand? And your homework book will be signed by your mother. Otherwise you will have to go and speak to the headmaster about it.

I turn away from him and go on with the lesson. I have won this round. There is no way he can defy me and get away with it, but I know that his hatred and rage have now redoubled and that I should expect trouble.

During playground duty I notice Leonardo and Matteo and a few others in a huddle on the far side of the playground. They are talking animatedly and turning from time to time to look at me and then returning to their discussion. Clearly I am part of whatever is going on. Leonardo is inciting them in some way against me. I can feel his hostility reaching across to me, his anger.

Ugo is waiting for me after school again, but I pretend not to notice him and go straight home. It has been raining again. After a quick lunch I put on my walking shoes and wrap myself up in warm clothes and a waterproof jacket and set out for a long walk, or as long as the island will permit. The path up the hill is very muddy with a stream running down the middle of it so that I am forced to walk on the side that has a slightly higher ridge. My shoes and socks are waterlogged within minutes and water drips off the brim of my hood on to my jacket and down my neck. My boots are soon heavy with clay. I stop from time to time to scrape the clay off against a pole or the support of one of the bare vines, but within seconds it is clinging to me again and hampering my progress.

When I get out on to the hilltop it grows easier. Here I have only to contend with the teeming rain and wind and I am soon soaked and cold, but it feels welcome to have bodily sensations after all those hours in the stuffy classroom. It takes me much longer to complete my usual walk, and it is already growing dark by the time I reach the headland and pass by the turn-off to Villa Circe. I see lights through the trees and smoke coming from the chimney but of course no one is outside in this weather. Only me.

But no, it is not only me.

Ugo has followed me up the hill. I had noticed him right from the beginning. I tried to ignore him at first and walk faster and faster, but he kept following me.

At last I stop and shout at him to go home. But when I turn a short while later, there he is still straggling up behind me in the rain. In the end I sit down on a rock and wait for him to reach me. Reluctantly, hesitantly, he comes closer.

– Ugo, you are going to have to stop following me like this. Do you understand? *Capisci*?

He stares at the ground.

– I'm your teacher, not your mother. I can't help you. You have to stay with your uncle and aunt.

He doesn't move, his eyes fixed on the same spot.

– I'm not angry with you, and I would like to help you, but I can't.

Still nothing.

– What do you want from me?

Silence.

– Go away! *Vai via*!

His eyes slip across my face then drop to the ground again.

– Now I'm going to go on walking and I don't want to see you following me any more. Do you understand?

But even as I speak I know it is useless. I resume my walk and in a few minutes hear his soft footsteps repeat after mine like an echo.

It is late afternoon when I make my way home, and the shadows are long. The sky has cleared and the last few clouds caught by the setting sun glow furiously red and pink against the deep blue of evening. I put my rucksack over one shoulder and begin the long walk back to the village, anxious to get home before it is completely dark. The soft footsteps still follow me, often stumbling, tired now, on the rough path.

But night comes early at this time of the year. The moon rises above the sea lighting my path and casting a long shadow behind me. It is pitch dark by the time I stumble down the last slope into the village. Everyone is already indoors, the sound of the news broadcast from the television set in every home disturbing the starry stillness of the night. The smell of frying garlic and tomatoes fills the alley. I open the door to my apartment and close it carefully behind me again. Home. I wonder if Ugo has found his way home safely, whether someone has given him something warm to eat, some dry clothes and a soft bed. I put my bag on the table and go to the bathroom to run a hot bath. I lie in the darkened room and soak the heat into my body, easing the stiff muscles and warming me so that I feel soft and sleepy. I wrap myself in a towel and go straight to bed where I fall into a deep sleep, a stunned hypnotic sleep full of disturbing dreams.

Tuesday 13 November

Friday, when I will have to return to the *Questura,* is drawing nearer.

I bought some persimmons today, soft, overripe, swollen autumnal fruits. I was passing through the square on my way home when my eye caught their outrageous roundness, the orange startling in the misty grey light, and I couldn't resist them. Ugo's aunt carefully put two into a brown paper bag for me and I carried them back home, but even so, by the time I got here they had both burst open and the flesh was seeping out on to the wrapping. I put them on a plate but it was not the same now that their perfection had been marred.

There was a parents-teachers meeting this evening, and I stayed late at school working afterwards. I had no inclination to go out into the windy town and to the loneliness of my room, preferring to stay here and mark the children's homework surrounded by the smell of chalk and ink.

When I finally stand up and stretch and prepare to leave I am surprised to notice that it is already nine o'clock. I let myself out of the side door, which the *bidello* has left on the latch for me, and walk along the road and into the square. It is abandoned at this time of night. The islanders retire early since they rise early to go out fishing or to work in the fields before sunrise. I have no fear alone here; there are no dangers on the island, it is too small and close-knit a community for that. A cat stands up from the shadows and approaches, meowing softly. I stoop and stroke its back, and it arches its body in pleasure to follow my hand, allowing itself to be caressed. It rolls over on to its back to offer me its belly to scratch. I don't like cats very much, they feel unclean to me, but I am moved by this gesture of companionship. It isn't just that she wants her back scratched – if that were all she could have rubbed her back up against a thorn bush.

As I stand up I become aware that there is another shape in the shadows. A human shape huddled against the wall, sleeping. I strain my eyes to make out the details in the dark, reluctant to go any closer. Could it be a vagrant, perhaps a drug addict come over from the mainland? A dog? It looks too small to be human. I take a step closer and suddenly realise it is a child's shape.

I straighten up. My first reaction is to turn away, to hasten my footsteps to my room, to close my door and switch on my light. I do not want this encounter in the dark, this contact with the unexpected that might drag me in. I draw myself up and walk to the alley leading up the hill to where I live. Then I stop, feeling drawn to go back. I feel a huge turmoil inside me that I do not want to give in to. Eventually I take control of myself and set off up the alley. I lock and bolt the door behind me and sit down on my bed. I don't switch on the light; I just lie on my bed fully dressed. I tell myself it is nothing important, that I don't need this in my life. Eventually I fall asleep.

Wednesday 14 November

I oversleep and arrive late at school. I find it difficult to be mentally present, my eyes feel puffy and sore. The children also seem subdued and sleepy. I notice Ugo hiding behind the shoulders of the child in front of him, head bowed, from his place near the back of the classroom. It crosses my mind that it could have been him last night, but then my attention is caught by one of the other children and the thought slips away unexplored.

Slowly the morning unfolds, the register is called, the homework taken in, marked exercises returned. I wonder why I bother to take so much time writing comments and correcting errors – the children never look at them, only at the mark they have been assigned. Ugo as usual has got a four. *Insufficiente* – *insuf* as the children say. It means he has done the work but not mastered the task. Today though he has not handed in his book. I have put him next to Irene, a quiet kind girl who I hope will be able to help him a little. I keep remembering the bundle in the corner of the square last night. His clothes are dishevelled – and I notice he is wearing the same clothes as yesterday. But then he often does. The same pair of worn jeans, a faded T-shirt under his *grembiule*, a grubby bomber jacket over the top. It feels as if he has been wearing them forever.

Thursday 15 November

Tomorrow I need to go over to the mainland and deal with *Ispettore* Lupo, but today is a public holiday. It is Remembrance Day. A platform has been erected in the square in front of the church and decked with flowers and purple drapes. People gather and stand around in little groups waiting. A misty day. The priest, in silver and purple robes, arrives surrounded by choirboys and deacons. Leonardo and Matteo are amongst them, dressed in white surplices. With perfect theatrical timing the priest mounts the stairs to the platform and begins to intone the *Requiem*, the mass of the dead, while the villagers kneel on the stone pebbles of the square. *Requiem aeternam dona eis, Domine* – Grant them eternal rest, O Lord, and let perpetual light shine upon them.

> *Absolve, Domine,*
> *animas omnium fidelium defunctorum*
> *ab omni vinculo delictorum*
> *Dies iræ! dies illa*
> *Solvet sæclum in favilla.*
> Forgive, O Lord,
> the souls of all the faithful departed
> from all the chains of their sins
> The day of wrath, that day
> Will dissolve the world in ashes.

After the Communion he descends and leads the procession of villagers down the road, the verger in front carrying the Madonna and cross, to the end of the village then up the hill in slow step, swathed in incense, a small brass band playing off-key, a tuba, a trumpet, a drum keeping time. Amongst the onlookers lining the road I notice Ugo, but he turns away as I pass and I do not see his eyes.

In front of the school we stop and gather about the priest. He climbs on to a pedestal so that he is raised above our heads. All the islanders gather closer, silent now, intent. Eyes are serious, even the young men usually so full of jokes and bravado, even the young girls proud in their beauty and freshness.

The bugler plays reveille. The priest turns and begins to read the names of the islanders who fell in the two world wars from the plaque on the wall. One by one they are named, as if for roll call, surname first, then name, and all the villagers, in a single voice, in unison, repeat '*presente*', answering for the dead, giving them a voice, holding them present in their midst.

– *Ariste Achille.*

– *Presente.*

– *Bernabei Luigi.*

– *Presente.*

– *Crisafulli Giovanni.*

– *Presente.*

There is no rush, no sense of time passing, no sense that this is an empty formality, the villagers united in remembering their dead. All thirty-three names are read, all thirty-three are found present and accounted for. One by one. Each is there. At the end the last post is sounded. The gathering breaks apart and the people, still in procession but lighter now, fragments of conversation rising here and there, return along the sandy road to the square where tables have been prepared with wine and food... later there will be dancing and bobbing for apples, and life will resume.

I return to my room.

As one of the schoolteachers, it is expected of me to take part. Part of my civic duties to the community. I hang to one side, shuffle along with the others, automatically repeating the words of the prayers I learned as a child in boarding school, finding the Italian translation of the words natural, calming, rounded on my tongue. I have done this each year for twenty years, followed the dusty road to the cemetery, the scruffy long yellowed grass stained darker yellow in places with yellow dandelions, the smell of incense and resin from the cypress trees mixed, the sun pale on my shoulders, the movement of my hair light around my face, against my cheek, the cry of the swallows gathering swift and fast in the sky before departing.

It strikes me that few people here except the very old men and women would have known any of those who died sixty-five and more years ago, except as brothers or sisters. Yet all wept for their naming, for their own death. The young mother imagining her own death, her orphaned child, her widowed husband. I try to imagine a world where I do not exist, a square, this square, without my presence, and find that the only way I can do it is by imagining myself hovering above it, the square seen from the vantage point of my eyes. It cannot just exist on its own. Or perhaps it could but I can't imagine it. Can't imagine a day, the blue sky speckled with tiny white clouds, the first intimation of rain, without feeling the cool breeze on my face, in my hair. On my body.

Friday 16 November
In the afternoon I go back to see *Ispettore* Lupo. Island to sea to bus to city to *Questura*. Each stage a transition.

The door is open and he is sitting at his desk. He sees me and beckons to me to come inside. The room smells faintly of brandy.

– *Entri. La stavo aspettando.* Come in. I was waiting for you.

I sit down on the bench against the wall.

He leans his chin on his hand and scrutinises me for a moment. He seems dangerously jovial today.

– *Allora, Signorina, è tornata, vedo. Brava.* You've come back. Good girl. So you have decided to collaborate with us?

He smiles.

– I still don't know what you want from me. I've done nothing wrong.

– Are you sure? Absolutely one hundred per cent sure that you've done nothing wrong? *Cento percento?* No guilt at all?

He sits back and smiles again.

– Why don't you just tell us everything. It would be much easier. Just tell us everything you know. We can't help you unless you tell us.

I don't say a word. He opens the drawer to pull out the pile of folders. I notice that the bottle is no longer there. He leans forward in his seat and opens the cover of the top folder. He picks up a photograph, examines it thoughtfully, then puts it down. Then, as if he has changed his mind, he picks it up again and holds it out to me. I reach forward to take it but he pulls back.

– *Non! Non si tocca.* You may not touch it.

I flinch and withdraw.

– What is it?

He holds it out again for me to see. A grainy black-and-white image. This time I make out two figures, two women photographed from behind. They are walking into a building, one following a few paces behind the other. They look familiar, something about the clothes, the hair. Suddenly I recognise them. It's Sabrina and me.

I sit back and close my eyes.

– *Vedo che si riconosce. Brava.*

I take a deep breath.

He laughs and raises his eyebrows, willing me to say something.

– *E allora...?*

– It could be me. But what is the problem with that? I have committed no crime.

– *È proprio sicura?*

He takes the last cigarette from the packet on his desk, crushes the packet in his fist and tosses it into a metal rubbish bin. My eyes follow it and I notice the empty brandy bottle beside it.

– What are you trying to insinuate?

– *Cosa mi dice di Angela Cremonesi?*

– I don't know anyone called Angela Cremonesi.

– The other woman in the photograph. *Si chiama Angela Cremonesi. La Cremonesi* is known to the police as a prostitute. She works near the main station. Her street name is Sabrina.

I shrug.

– So what is that to me?

– She often takes her clients to the *Pensione Arcadia*.

– I still don't know where you are trying to go with this.

– This picture shows you going into the *pensione* with her. What is there between you? Are you paying her for sex? It could be a criminal offence, you know.

His eyes drop to my breasts and linger there.

I stand up.

– All you have here is a picture of me from behind going into a nondescript building and you have come to all sorts of conclusions. I don't know what you are thinking, but I'm going. You're wasting my time.

He smiles.

– *Si sieda. Non abbiamo ancora finito.* Not so fast, *Signorina.* We haven't finished yet. Sit down.

I sit.

– We are watching you, *Signorina.* Something is going on and we want to know what it is. You will please come back next Friday. We have more talking to do.

I wander down to the Roman ruins. There is a bench and I sit down. There are dozens of cats sunning themselves in the golden afternoon sunlight. I open my handbag and catch sight of a small parcel wrapped in white-and-silver paper. For some reason the sight of it bothers me. Without removing it from my bag I unwrap it. Inside it is a knife. I touch it, running my hand along the handle, touching the hard, cold blade. I wonder where it comes from.

A man sits down on the bench beside me, a small round man with a bald head.

– *Permesso?* he says companionably. He stretches his arm along the back of the bench. I nod although I would rather be alone. He laughs.

– *Ma guarda quei gatti.* He points and I follow the line of his finger to where two cats are mating.

The hand moves off the back of the bench and, as if it were the most natural thing in the world, slips on to my shoulder.

– *Guarda come le piace, alla gattaccia.* Look at how much she likes it, the filthy she-cat.

He hesitates a moment.

– *Anche a te piace?* Do you also like it?

He puts his hand on my thigh, bends closer and with his lips touching my ear whispers roughly.

– *Anche tu gridi così?* Do you also scream like that?

I don't reply.

He takes my hand and leads me to a crowded *caffè* across the road where he orders a grappa standing up at the counter. By now his arm is around my waist. He pays, drinks, and guides me to his car parked nearby. We get inside. He pulls me to him, already busy unbuttoning his fly, then pushes my head down into his lap. I hear him gasp as he fills my mouth.

Before he is spent we are interrupted by a traffic policeman who knocks officiously on the window and tells us to move on. The man drives a short way to a park with a lake. From a public telephone booth he phones a friend and arranges to borrow his apartment for the afternoon. In exchange, he says, the friend can also have some fun.

Saturday 17 November

Sunday 18 November

Monday 19 November

By Monday morning I am ready to go back to school although my lips are bruised and it is painful to walk. Ugo is not there. I eat two eggs and green salad. I wonder what Ugo is doing, if he will come back to school tomorrow.

Tuesday 20 November

School. English history, Henry VIII and his wives. Ugo is not there.

In the latest box of books was a copy of Erasmus of Rotterdam's *In Praise of Folly*. I prefer the Italian title, *Elogio della follia* – In Praise of Madness. I like the word madness better. I will read that one next.

Avvocato Rossi had interesting tastes in literature; this box is a source of great delight to me. I wonder what else is in there. Perhaps this weekend I should unpack it and see what else I will find.

There was another letter from the police today. After school I put it on top of the fridge on top of the others. I make minestrone soup for supper – the apartment is full of the smell of onions and vegetables.

Wednesday 21 November

School. Where has Ugo gone? He has not been at school for several days now. I first noticed he was missing on Monday when I handed out the homework books and was left holding his scruffy, dog-eared one, which always stood out from the others. I look carefully around the room amongst the heads bent over their work in the white electric light that struggles against the pale colourless glare that filters through the window leaving no place for shadows, just an irritable sense of exposure. I do not fill in the register until the end of the lesson in the hope that Ugo might still arrive, but at last I am forced to mark a capital A for absent against his name. I am not quite sure why I feel disturbed by this, but I do. He has never been absent before this week.

At the end of the day I take my register down to the office and leave a note for the secretary to call the family. The school has a policy that the family should be contacted after the third consecutive absence.

On my way to school the next morning, I make a detour past the vegetable market. The stall-keepers are all huddled around small braziers in the crisp morning air. I catch sight of Ugo's uncle, massive and bloated in a frayed black-and-white checked pullover, stamping his feet in outsize rubber boots and whistling to himself with his hands in his pockets. His face is red and unshaven, unkempt. His wife, in a faded torn overall, is weighing out some tomatoes for an early customer, a mark of blood red against the grey of the morning light. They both look absorbed and I hasten my step and walk on to school without saying a word.

There is no sign of Ugo.

After lunch I go out for a walk. The weather is mild, overcast but with the clouds breaking from time to time and brilliant blue sky opening behind it. I have not taken any exercise for days and I feel quite breathless as I walk up the slope, but I soon find my second wind, as my mother used to call it. I decide to walk along the cliffs to clear my head. I know I don't have much time as the sun sets early now and I do not want to find myself stumbling about in the dark. I choose a narrow muddy path behind the village that threads its way along the edge of the fields and then begins to climb through the tangled underbrush. As always on the edges of human habitation there is an area of transition, where a discarded shoe, a shard of glass, a plastic doll, slowly decompose. I note these details as I walk, feeling distaste. But then, as I reach the top of the cliff and the horizon opens out, I breathe deeply again and take in the aromatic scent of the mimosa. I can see the path that follows across the top of the cliffs, then moves away from the sea to cut across the saddle and climb again to the highest peaks. I listen for the sound of Ugo's step but all I hear is the wind snagging against the bushes and the sound of the seagulls high above calling, calling, calling.

Friday 23 November

Friday again and I know I should go to the *Questura* but I don't have the energy to take ferries and buses and negotiate the busy city streets. If *Ispettore* Lupo wants to see me he will have to come and fetch me himself.

Saturday 24 November

I am so tired, my body feels exhausted as if I had taken a great battering, yet I have done nothing out of the ordinary.

I stay up marking homework until late. I have nothing else to do. It fills the empty space between dinner and when I feel I can legitimately go to bed. I have no reason to wait until eleven o'clock to go to bed, but this has become my routine and I try not to vary it since it upsets my metabolism.

Sunday 25 November

I do not let anyone into my room. I lock it each time I leave. Even Signora Bruna does not enter.

But today Ugo knocked.

It is late in the evening, a rainy cold day, the sea and sky the colour of gunmetal. The ferry has not been able to venture into the harbour because of the high seas. I have spent the evening as usual at Modugno's *trattoria*, I ordered *pasta e lenticchie* followed by cheese and salad. I have had more to drink than I should have and am feeling sleepy and irritable by the time I get home. I am sitting in my armchair in front of the window when suddenly I hear a gentle tapping at my door. At first I do not even recognise it as a knocking; I think it must be a branch scratching against the wall or a sound from my neighbour's room. But then it comes again, and then a third time. I pull on a jacket and go down to the street and open the door a crack. Outside, soaking wet, wild-eyed, is Ugo, teeth chattering, a black eye. As I stand in front of him there on the threshold, I see him wavering as if he were about to faint.

I don't know what to do. I can't send him back to his uncle, but nor do I want to get involved. I feel reluctant to take him to the police station, because I know I will have to make an official statement and I am afraid of the judgemental eyes of officialdom in my little world. *Ispettore* Lupo's face flashes through my mind.

I should have turned the boy away, shut the door tight, and sent him back to his uncle. I knew it would mean trouble to take him in. Yet I couldn't help myself. Something in me reached out to him and brought him inside. I put my arm around his shoulders and under his knees and carried him up to the warmth of my room.

I bring him to my room. I remove his dirty jacket and trousers, his ragged T-shirt. He lets me do what I want, eyes averted. I bring him a towel and an old tracksuit of mine and I clothe him in it. It is too big for him but I suppose it doesn't matter. There is no one to see. I take his clothes and wring them out, noticing as I do how threadbare they are, and hang them over the radiator to dry.

His body does not soften or shape itself as I move it; he remains rigid and hard, yet I know he is aware of me, is opposing me, opposing my soft touch. I, who struggle to be soft, have to force this upon him. I shudder at the bruises and cigarette burns I discover on his arms and chest.

– Who did this?

He doesn't answer.

– Was it your uncle?

He doesn't answer.

I take a soft cloth and warm soapy water and gently wipe his limbs, his chest, his legs, trying to soothe, trying to soften the hurt. I hug his body to mine, then, fearing his reaction, I begin to wipe his face, first his forehead, the sweatiness of his brow and up into the short cropped hair. I outline the shape of his brows and, having squeezed out the cloth with clean fresh water, I wash his eyes, tenderly, afraid to give him more pain.

Monday 26 November

I go to school again this morning, leaving Ugo still asleep in my bed. I put a few biscuits on a plate for him to eat if he wakes up, but I do not have the heart to wake him myself. I find it difficult to concentrate on the lessons. There are feelings of excitement and dread rippling through me, alternating. When I get home he is gone. I stroll down to the market later and see him, dressed in his dry clothes, helping his uncle out as usual.

He notices me and moves away and I do not follow. I buy some tomatoes and *scarola* from his uncle, who looks at me, small eyes unblinking, impenetrable. I wonder whether he knows. What Ugo has told him. I pay and leave. I hear him sniggering as I cross the square, but do not turn to see what it is he is laughing at.

Tuesday 27 November
I could not sleep last night.

Wednesday 28 November
I still can't sleep. I will go mad unless I sleep.

Thursday 29 November
Three days have passed, days of anxiety, of fear, yet how can I tell you of the stirrings of joy and life in me. All my instincts tell me I should not let him come back again, yet I know I will not be able to turn him away if he returns.

And late last night he came. I was walking home from Modugno's where I had seen his uncle drinking with his friends when I heard his soft footsteps behind me again.

– Ugo, I call without turning my head.

Silence.

The echoing footsteps falter then stop. My heart drops but I keep walking. I turn into the alleyway and then I hear them again, faster now, trying to catch up, anxious not to lose me.

– Ugo, I call again. Come upstairs and I'll make you some camomile tea.

Still no reply. I put the key in the lock and turn it and push open the door. As I am about to close it he appears on the doorstep looking distressed. I walk up the steep stairs, aware of his uncertain presence behind me. He comes inside. I light a candle, not wanting to frighten him with the bright neon light of the room. I hand him a bottle of birdseed and ask him to fill the feeder.

With great care and attention he lifts the cage from its hook, tongue sticking out from concentration, careful not to upset anything or hurt the little bird, which flaps agitatedly but stays on its perch. He pulls out the little drawer and fills it with seed, then replaces it. He washes out the water bowl which is quite empty and refills that too. The little bird jumps off its perch and goes to drink, sipping from the bowl and then lifting its head to swallow.

In the meantime I make some tea and toast with butter and honey. The smell of flowers fills the room.

– Come and sit down now and eat.

– *Posso far uscire l'uccellino*?

I nod, and he opens the door of the cage and puts his hand inside. With great delicacy he takes the *cardellino* in his hand and brings it out. He sits down and opens his hand. The bird does not move but eyes him curiously. Ugo takes a bite of toast then puts a crumb on his hand and holds it out for the bird on his palm. It looks at him, then darts forward and pecks up the crumb.

– *Guarda. Hai visto*, he says excitedly. *Ha mangiato.*

– I think it likes toast.

– *Pensi che gli piaccia.*

I smile.

– Of course it likes you.

We sit in silence, the three of us. He strokes the little bird's back and breast with his short stubby fingers with the nails chewed down to the quick. He is not a beautiful child but to me this evening he feels infinitely beautiful. At last it is time to go to bed.

– Where are you going to sleep tonight?

The guarded look comes over his face again. He shrugs. He puts the bird back into its cage and closes the door.

– Can you go home?

He shakes his head violently and gazes at the floor.

– What then?

For a while there is no reply, and then he mumbles:

– *Posso restare qui*? Can I stay here?

I know I shouldn't, that it will bring only trouble. But I can't send him out again to sleep in the street or to face his drunken uncle.

– OK. But just for tonight. OK?

He nods.

– Then help me make up the stretcher here for you.

– *Posso dormire nel tuo letto*? Can I sleep in your bed?

I cannot say no.

We climb into the bed and cling there together like castaways.

Friday 30 November

In the morning I wake him early and help him to get dressed. I give him a handful of biscuits and see him to the door, afraid of the watchful eye of the islanders who will read something perverse into the relationship, of this I am sure. I open the door, look up and down the alley, and check the windows. The shutters are all still closed but that doesn't mean anything – Signora Bruna is an expert at spying through the cracks of closed shutters – and push him into the street. When I go to school later I see him sitting on the edge of the dock dangling his feet over the edge. He lifts his hand and waves and I waggle my fingers in return and wink. I see his face light up in a smile.

I pretend not to notice him in class but I am constantly aware of him on the periphery of my vision, the emotional centre of the room for me.

I know I should be careful. I know implicitly, without even needing to think about it, that no one should know that I have taken him in, and that he has slept in my bed. I know it must not happen again. Yet I feel such sweetness when I think of his arms around me and mine around him, his head on my shoulder.

Saturday 1 December

I ate some salad and cheese.

Sunday 2 December

Monday 3 December
Ugo came again last night.

Tuesday 4 December

Wednesday 5 December
Ugo. Polenta and mushrooms.

Thursday 6 December
Lentil soup and salad. I know there is something I am supposed
to do tomorrow but I can't remember what it is. Ugo came.

Friday 7 December
I almost forgot it is Friday and I have to go to the *Questura* after
school. I haven't thought of Lupo all week and can't remember
why he wants to see me. By the time I reach my classroom I am
wide awake. I decide to take the children outside into the fresh
air for their lesson. The morning is far too beautiful to waste
indoors in the stuffy centrally heated classroom. It takes longer
than I thought to get them all ready in their hats and jackets
and gloves. We set off at last, the children walking two by two
holding hands, with me leading the party. Where am I going to
take them? What am I going to teach them? I have no idea. I had
thought of teaching them a song, perhaps 'Speed Bonnie Boat',
seeing we are doing the Stuarts in history and they love singing.
Singing is very good for them. It helps with their pronunciation
of the often difficult English sounds. The air is so clear today
that I can see the snowy white on the peaks of the mountains
far in the distance across the sea. Even Vesuvius has a white tip.
It is bitterly cold and I feel the chill bite into my cheeks, turning
them pink and my nose red. Too late I realise it is too cold for an
outdoor lesson and that anyway we would need a blackboard
for me to write the words of the song on. I turn the lesson into
an active clapping game instead but by now my enthusiasm and
energy are waning and after a few more minutes I lead them
back to the classroom that in contrast to the brightness looks

even more drab and overheated than usual. I write the words of the song in big letters on the blackboard and tell them to copy it into their exercise books. They are restless now and I hear them fidgeting and giggling behind my back, but when I turn I see only blank faces. They take ages and the bell rings while they are still copying down the words. We will have to leave the song until another day.

I put away my books and clean the board carefully, then take the register back to the office and set off home. The children are also still in the streets reluctant to go home and be inside again. I feel something hit my sleeve and look down. It is a paper bullet from a blowpipe. The boys all have them. I wonder if this came from Leonardo or Matteo. I look around quickly but no one is taking any notice of me. All are talking or minding their own business and I am forced to just pretend that nothing has happened and carry on walking. I hasten my step now, anxious to get home and away from these hostile eyes. I climb the stairs with a sense of oppression. I pack a bag and take the ferry to Anzio.

Ispettore Lupo is not at the *Questura* today. His colleague tells me that he has taken a few days off work.

I haven't had anything to eat, so I find an inexpensive-looking *trattoria* near the station and order the dish of the day without knowing what it is. It turns out to be tripe. I push it to one side and focus on the salad and bread.

I wait until ten o'clock when I feel sure that Sabrina will be working. I walk along the porticoes. Quite a few of the women are out, mostly middle-aged women who look as if they would be more comfortable sitting at home knitting in front of the television, watching over the restless sleep of their grandchildren in the makeshift bed in the corridor. Men hover in the shadows, whether clients or protectors is not clear. I wonder if *Ispettore* Lupo is there too, watching me, wanting me, seeking my scent. It feels as if it is too late now to worry about things like that.

A car stops and Sabrina alights and the customer drives off

alone into the night. It takes her a minute or so to regain her composure, to repair the shell of her face. She straightens her clothes, reapplies her smudged make-up, then turns and sees me watching her from the far pavement across the dark street. I gesture and she nods and sets off towards the small hotel. I follow. We slip off our clothes in the half-darkness of the room and climb into the over-soft bed. She strokes me gently, holding me tight as if I were a small child, and I find myself sobbing, my body racked with violent sobs that I can't control. I want to tell her about Ugo, about the sweetness of him, about my fear of what the islanders would say if they knew. But I know instinctively that she will also not understand, that she will also judge, and so I stay silent. Her hands keep smoothing me, defining my skin, my forms, the boundaries of my self, softly, rhythmically reconstituting my surface that feels so battered, circling my breasts and then down into those funny places, touching softly, gently, until I feel the flood upon me. I fall asleep at last in her arms amidst the smell of sweat and damp sheets.

Saturday 8 December

She is gone when I awake and I am alone. The morning light is creeping through the green shutters. I have a shower then return to the large bed where I lie propped up on the pillows like a child who has cried herself out. Then, feeling numb, I pull on my clothes that still carry the smell of rancid oil from last night's restaurant. I step into my damp shoes, put my bag over my shoulder and open the door. The owner is sweeping the hallway. I step over a used condom, and recover my identity card from the chain-smoking concierge who is listening to the soccer on a tiny transistor radio.

I catch a passing bus and, as it trundles heavily in front of a church, on a sudden whim I press the button to tell the driver I want to get off. I walk back to the church and push open the door. It is dark inside, only a few candles flickering below an ex-voto painting of the Madonna and Child. I sit down on a pew at the back wondering what on earth I am doing here.

I become aware in the silence and dark that I am not alone, that above me in the shadows someone is moving. I listen carefully; it sounds as if whoever it is is turning pages. Then I hear a squeaking puffing sound.

The music starts, slow and soft. How do I describe what it sounds like to hear an organ in a darkened church unexpectedly? I sit back in the pew and close my eyes. The man above me, for I have decided it must be a man from the energy with which he plays, fumbles, stops, clears his throat, then goes back to the beginning of the bar and tries again. Again at the same place in the music his fingers falter and get stuck, again he stops and goes back. How well I remember just that, the striving for perfection, for the note to be just right. I feel tears streaming down my face and I am glad it is dark and no one can see me.

My eyes settle back on the Madonna and Child in the dark chapel above me. All but one of the candles have gone out. I stand up, take some money from my purse and put it into the offerings box. I take three candles and light them from the spluttering remains of the last candle. The painting lights up in the flickering golden light.

My thoughts go to Ugo.

How many hours have I been sitting there? I have no idea. The organist has long since gone, it is dark outside. The rain has stopped and the air is soft and warm and fragrant. It feels full of promise. Dolphins accompany our little vessel back across the straits to Ponza, gleaming white in the moonlight as their backs surface alongside the boat. They seem to be playing with us as they swim around and under the hull, or surf behind us in our wake. I remember stories of shipwrecked sailors being saved and carried to shore by these creatures and I feel my chest and throat opening with love and wonder at the beauty of the natural world. They turn back as we pass the breakwater and round the light at the end of the harbour wall. It is late and there are only a few stragglers to meet us, but I see a childish form flit aside in the shadows and make out Ugo's crew cut and round face. I collect my bags and come ashore. I know he is waiting for me, and that he will follow me. I pretend not to notice him, but find myself smiling to myself as I walk along the jetty and up the *Lungomare* to the village.

Sunday 9 December
We spend the day quietly together reading and telling each other stories. In the evening after dinner I send him home.

Monday 10 December
The alarm clock wakes me as usual. It is still dark and will stay dark until after I have got to school, I know. The weather has changed and a thin cold wind from Siberia has started blowing across the sea. It seems to manage to penetrate through the bricks of the walls, through the chinks in the plaster, and I shiver as I pull on my clothes, warm woollen polo-necked sweater and warm trousers, boots, a heavy jacket and gloves. I would wear a hat too, but can't find it, so I give up at the last minute and go out bareheaded. The cold catches my cheeks and filters down the neck of my jacket, then is stopped by the collar of my sweater. My cheeks are pink, I am sure, by the time I reach my classroom.

The room is overheated and stuffy, but I don't dare open the windows for fear that one of the children might catch cold. I sit at my desk and give them a dictation, the longest I can find to take up the whole lesson. It is a passage from Robert Louis Stevenson from their textbooks. The children keep interrupting, wanting me to repeat what I have just read, clearly struggling to understand and reproduce the sounds. I wonder what they can be making of Jekyll, of this complex fictitious world so very remote from their own, or from mine either.

I read the lines slowly, repeating the chunks of words twice to allow them time to write in between, so making it even more incomprehensible:

It was a fine, / clear, / January day, / wet under foot / where the frost / had melted, / but cloudless overhead; / and the Regent's

Park / was full / of winter chirrupings / and sweet / with spring odours. / I sat in the sun / on a bench; / the animal within me / licking the chops of memory; / the spiritual side / a little drowsed, / promising subsequent penitence, / but not yet moved / to begin. / After all, / I reflected, / I was like my neighbours; / and then I smiled, / comparing myself / with other men, / comparing my active goodwill / with the lazy cruelty / of their neglect. / And at the very moment / of that vain-glorious thought, / a qualm / came over me, / a horrid nausea / and the most deadly shuddering. / These passed away, / and left me faint; / and then / as in its turn / the faintness subsided, / I began to be aware / of a change / in the temper / of my thoughts, / a greater boldness, / a contempt of danger, / a solution of the bonds / of obligation. / I looked down; / my clothes hung formlessly / on my shrunken limbs; / the hand that lay / on my knee / was corded / and hairy. / I was once more / Edward Hyde. / A moment before / I had been safe / of all men's respect, / wealthy, / beloved / – the cloth laying for me / in the dining-room / at home; / and now I was / the common quarry / of mankind, / hunted, / houseless, / a known murderer, / thrall to the gallows./

The passage disturbs me, although I am not quite sure why. I contemplate, wonder briefly if the people who compile these textbooks understand what they are putting into them. Who on earth would choose this passage, and for what possible reason?

The morning drags by in a sequence of dreary disappointments, repetitions of other mornings almost identical to this one, almost but not quite, of boredom and irritation and resentment. All the feelings of love and hope that I felt yesterday have evaporated, leaving just a sour irritability in their place. At last the final bell rings. I pack up my books, clean the blackboard, put away the chalk and leave the room. I drop the register off in the office. The headmaster is there with Cappi. They fall silent as I enter. The headmaster nods at me, then watches me wordlessly as I pack away the register and leave.

It is still freezing cold outside, the difference from the day

before as extreme as if I had flown to a different continent. The sky is dark and heavy with clouds, and the sea heaves with long-submerged currents although the surface is unbroken and lies opaque and unreflecting like an oil slick over the water. I need some fresh air after hours confined in the overheated room so I walk out on to the breakwater breathing in the cold damp iodine smell but even that is not enough to lift the sense of stifling claustrophobia that grips my chest and diaphragm. I linger there for a while until it grows too cold for me to stay any longer and I walk back to my apartment. There's a note, in large, childish handwriting stuck to my door.
– *Troia.*
– Slut.

Tuesday 11 December
I am sure it must be Leonardo. What does he know? Can he have seen Ugo arriving at my apartment or leaving in the morning? I close my shutters tight and go to bed early.

Wednesday 12 December
A violent storm with white sheets of lightning shatters across the sky and the sea is very wild. Huge waves crash against the breakwater and thunder through my dreams. Several of the little boats break their moorings in the night and are dragged out to the sea, which sucks and pulls at the rocks. Dark currents swirl perilously just below the surface as if there were huge monsters moving in the watery blackness. The lighthouse on the point howls mournfully as its light spins round and round trying to penetrate the gloom.

A body was washed up on the rocks this morning, in the sea-weed, sucked down, tugged down, hair afloat, stomach awash.

Like everyone else, I go to see. An illegal immigrant on a night crossing from North Africa, full of hope for a better future, or perhaps a prostitute after a quarrel with a client. Waves lapping gently rock the body, which is naked, protective tattoos cut into her cheeks and forehead, loose belly with the dark shadow of pubic hair. I watch as the rescue workers lift the limp form on to the stretcher, an arm trailing lifelessly over the side, seaweed slicked over her face. I want to remove it so she can breathe again, but it will take more, much more than that, to make her breathe. First she will need to dissolve, to disintegrate, her organs disintegrating, the cells decomposing, the molecules separating and then being reabsorbed, to regenerate in some other form, perhaps as air, perhaps as a rain cloud, an ice crystal frozen for eternity. I sit on a rock and watch, the waves lap-lapping at my feet. I feel life through my flesh but also death as I feel the shame of her public nakedness when her thighs fall apart and the boys giggle, excited and aroused.

Waves generated by the pull of wind and moon, generate degenerate. The salty smell, the seaweed smell, the smell of breaking waters, returning to the amniotic waters, to the holding, floating warmth, the lungs filled with fluid. Sightless eyes, there is nothing to see, tiny fishes have nibbled her nose, her eyes, her lips, featureless foetal face, flat, bleached, bloodless. But she has no longer any connection, no umbilical cord attaching her to a life source.

Thursday 13 December

The stranger left this morning.

I am sitting in my classroom in exactly the same position as when he arrived last month. That feels like a lifetime away, a world of innocence. So much seems to have happened in the meantime. The taxi redeposits him with his suitcases on the jetty where the ferry is already waiting to depart. With a strange indifference I watch him go, as if he no longer has any part in my life. And indeed it is many days since I last thought of him. I wonder about that. It is since Ugo came.

I also received a phone call from *Ispettore* Lupo. There is something about his voice that alarms me, although I can't pin it down. He says he wants to see me, asks me to come back tomorrow. Polite. Cold. Not bullying.

I am not hungry.

Friday 14 December

At the *Questura, Ispettore* Lupo is sitting at his desk and appears to be waiting for me. My file is open in front of him and he is squinting at one of the pages in the yellow light of the small desk lamp. His movements are as slow and spiderlike as on the previous occasions, but I sense an excitement beneath the surface that worries me. His colleague is sitting across the room on the plastic chair.

– *Ah, è Lei.*

I nod in greeting and sit down on the chair in front of him. He stares at me for a moment.

– *Come Le ho detto l'altra volta, abbiamo chiesto il Nulla Osta alle autorità sudafricane.* As you know, we asked the consulate for your police record. *Ecco, ora è arrivato.* It has arrived. Of course you understand that this is just a routine check because of the murder. You have nothing to worry about.

He looks at me again with that thin-lipped smile.

– Do you?

– Do I what?

– Have anything to worry about?

I don't answer. I don't know where this is leading.

– *Hanno mandato anche altre cartelle.* They have also sent other folders. They evidently think they are relevant.

I start and turn my face away so that he will not see my eyes, certain that I will not be able to conceal my expression. What have they sent? What I have dreaded all these years has finally come to pass. But he seems not to notice, and continues talking.

– *Le studieremo nei prossimi giorni.* We will examine them in the next few days. You must please be available to come back so that we can talk. Also, we need your fingerprints. Before you leave today you must go downstairs to Room 14 where they will take your prints.

I nod.

He looks back at me with his pale eyes, and then taps on the file with his index finger.

– Your records are very interesting.

My breath catches in my throat.

He winks at his colleague.

– They have sent some very interesting things. *La cartella clinica pure.* And your hospital folder too. You didn't tell me about that, now did you. So interesting.

He sniggers and rubs his hands together, a cold dry sound like the sound of wind through long dry grass.

– Don't you want to know what they say? Come back next Friday and we can look at them together. *Dobbiamo parlare ancora.*

I feel their eyes on my legs as I leave the room.

I scrub my hands to remove the ink in the dirty bathroom next to the waiting room and then go out into the street.

Ispettore Lupo's questions and insinuations trouble me deeply. I walk past the *Pensione Arcadia* on my way back. It still feels familiar to me, but I still have no memory of it. I make my way to the nearest bar across the street from which I can see the entrance. There is only one small round table with two chairs squashed up in the corner. I sit down. There are coffee stains and spilt sugar on the Formica table top. I order some tea and open the well-paged copy of *La Repubblica* in front of me to avoid having to meet anyone's eyes or exchange banter with the barman.

I know I have been there before.

I try to imagine what it would be like if I rang the bell of the *pensione* and went through the door off the street.

I can picture it clearly. I know the door will open on to a deep, high-ceilinged, echoing hallway with an ancient lift shaft in a metal cage at the far end. Five wide stone steps will lead up to the left. At the top will be a glass door with the words *Pensione Arcadia* embossed on it in chipped gold letters. If you open the door, a little bell will ring somewhere in the recesses of the building. There will be a residual ingrained smell of tomatoes and garlic over another slightly mouldy smell of badly dried linen. There will be a desk and a row of pigeonholes against the wall, each with a number, some with the room keys hanging below the number, the patron no doubt sleeping late, still occupying the room. There will be, I know it, a brass bell on the counter to call someone's attention, although your presence has already been signalled by the bell triggered as you crossed the threshold. If you go back out on to the landing, you will be able to choose either to take the lift up to your level, or to climb the narrow flight of grimy stairs as it spirals around the lift shaft, up to your room. When you reach the landing, there will be four doors. Yours is the one on the right, at the head of the stairs.

Can I prove myself wrong? Should I go in and see whether this could be true? I could ring the bell and speak to the concierge, ask if he recognises me, find an excuse to look around, tell him that I lost an earring, could it still be in the room under the bed perhaps? Hopefully he will take me up.

Yet how can I tell you what dread I feel? What if it is as I say? What if he does recognise me? Then I will have to face up to the knowledge that I am not able to remember. That my body was there although I was not. I decide that I do not want that certainty. There are levels of truth that I find unbearable. I pay for my tea and go out into the street, determined to return to the station.

But somehow I find myself retracing my steps along the pavement until I am standing outside the *Pensione Arcadia* once more, my hand raised to press the bell. I hesitate for a moment, but only for a moment do I manage to wrest control over myself, then my finger presses the white porcelain knob and I stand waiting in the leaden cold. A woman's voice rasps through an intercom.

– *Chi è?* Who's there?

I mumble something in reply and the door clicks open.

I push open the heavy wooden door, pass inside and let it go with a slam at my shoulders. I am in a dark deep hallway, with the lift shaft at the end exactly where I knew it would be. With a heavy heart I climb the five shallow stone steps to the left and push open the glass door. I recognise the smell. I recognise the little bell on the counter, the row of pigeonholes against the wall.

A woman is standing waiting. A woman about forty, plump, with angry suspicious-looking eyes, dressed in black, a few black hairs sprouting from her upper lip and chin. I know her face but can remember nothing about her. I had not expected her. I am not sure whether I have seen her before. I have a faint recollection of a man, middle-aged with a paunch, then the image wobbles and fades. I try to clutch at it but it is gone.

– *Mi dica*, the woman says curtly.

I quickly invent a story. I explain that I stayed here a few weeks ago, that I lost my ring.

   – Has anything been found?

   – No.

   – There was a man here. Can I speak to him?

She interrupts me at once.

   – *Non c'è*. He's not here.

   – Will he be back later?

   – *Non c'è*, she repeats. *È morto*.

I understand that she is not prepared to say anything more.

I thank her and leave. The heavy door slams behind me with a bang.

Saturday 15 December

Sunday 16 December

I spend a restless night tossing and turning in my bed. Whenever I fall asleep I have ragged dreams, from which I awaken gasping, of gaping laughing mouths, tongues poking in and out obscenely, eyes mocking and cruel. I feel sure that there was someone watching me in the alley the other night when I opened the door to the child.

Who was it and what could he know about me? Even if it was *Ispettore* Lupo he could only track my outer life. He would still know nothing about my private thoughts, or anything about the boy. But I don't know what information he has got from the South African authorities. What records do the doctors, the police, store from those times of which I have no memory? What would they know of my inner world?

Towards morning I fall into a deep sleep, so deep that I don't hear my alarm clock, or the morning sounds of the harbour.

Monday 17 December

I startle awake a few minutes before the school bell and drag on my clothes. I hear the bell ring as I rush down the alley and across the square. The children are already inside. I stop at the door. I have never seen them so animated. The boys have fabricated a ball of paper and sticky tape and are playing a kind of basketball between the desks. The girls are banging on the wooden desk tops with their open hands as an accompaniment to a song they are singing in chorus, over and over.

> *Sant'Antonio, Sant'Antonio*
> *Il nemico del demonio.*

Without pausing, and increasing the tempo and volume, they sing it again.

> *Sant'Antonio, Sant'Antonio*
> *Il nemico del demonio.*

The noise is deafening and they don't notice my arrival at the door. It is only when I cross the room to the podium that they become aware of my presence.

They slowly settle, scrutinising me carefully for signs of anger or retaliation. I lean against the lectern watching them. A tense silence falls. I let it lie there between us, enjoying their fear. At last I tell them to sit.

The lesson falls into its usual pattern: homework is distributed, I repeat my explanation of the working of the adjective in English and its position in relation to the noun. I notice the stifled yawns, the dull eyes. I send one of the children to the office to fetch the register. She returns holding the big green book and an envelope for me. I glance at it quickly. Just a plain white envelope. I ask the child:

– Who gave you this?

She shrugs and looks at me sullenly, without understanding. I repeat my question in Italian.

– *Da dove viene?*

She points down the corridor and giggles with embarrassment, but still says nothing. I give up.

After the morning's lessons, I sit at my desk feeling limp and exhausted. I take the envelope between my fingers and turn it over, but it is blank. Eventually I take a pencil and slit it open carefully. Inside is a sheet of paper and a photograph. I have a horrible feeling about the photograph and quickly place it face down on the table. With a sense of foreboding I open the letter. Blank. No name. No signature. No possibility of reply. I feel my heart beating fast. With trembling fingers I turn over the photograph. A grainy black-and-white image, but there is no mistaking the faces. Ugo and I stand in the alley as I unlock the door into my apartment. I have an anxious look on my face.

I tear the photograph into tiny pieces and place them back inside the envelope.

I tell Ugo he must not come again. Ever. I see his face drain of blood and he reels out of the classroom.

Tuesday 18 December
What I knew would happen all along has finally come to pass. It could not have come at a worse time.

The headmaster sent one of the pupils to my classroom this morning with a message asking me to come to his office during the lunch break. When I enter he is sitting at his vast polished desk with the Italian flag to one side. He half rises, nods at me to take a chair on the other side of the desk, then lowers himself carefully to the edge of his seat and clears his throat.

He goes about the matter with great circumstance and self-importance, puffing himself up, filling himself with the words. He speaks about the Ministry in Rome, about the *Provveditorato,* about IRRSAE. About policy regarding qualifications, unions, board examinations, the democratic values of the republic, language policy. At last he comes to the matter at hand.

A teacher has been appointed – a person of the highest calibre, you understand. A real teacher. He will be arriving at the end of the month. From the first of February my services will no longer be required. He wants to take this opportunity to thank me for all my years of hard work, what was it, five, six years? He seems surprised when I tell him it is almost twenty. As a temporary teacher I have always existed only on the periphery of his vision, a shadow without clear outline or colour.

He gets up and accompanies me to the door.

I come back to my empty classroom. The children are still outside playing in the pale winter sunshine. The air is stuffy. I stand at the window looking out at the playground and the hills beyond, my eyes unfocused. Strange that I can feel so indifferent.

The afternoon goes by in a haze. Ugo is not in class. I give the children an exercise to keep them busy.

It is growing dark by the time I leave the school buildings and make my way up the narrow streets to the old town where I lodge. It feels like years since I was last here. I go upstairs and lie down on my back on the bed and stare up at the ceiling. A fly is circling round and round the naked light bulb that hangs blankly from its wire. The eyes in the paintings that surround me leer at me mockingly. I feel my head spinning, and my stomach lurches. I try to turn over but the room sways about me. I try to get to the bathroom, but all I can do is slip off the bed on to the cold tile floor and attempt to crawl there, but then the floor feels so cool and my body so hot that I just lie down and let myself go.

It is night-time when I awake, still lying on the cold floor, my body stiff and frozen. I try to get up but my head throbs violently and at last I give up. I am afraid I am very sick, that I need a doctor, that I am going to die, but the thoughts just keep slipping away. I have a sudden image of a long dormitory with rows of beds marching down each side of the room, each bed below a high barred window, the moonlight shining through, casting barred shadows across the beds and over the sleeping drugged bodies of the women lying there. I don't know how long I lie there. At some point I drag myself to my bed and fall into a deep sleep.

Wednesday 19 December

It is late morning when I wake up. I get up and wash, then make some tea and go back to bed. By the afternoon I feel a little better. I eat some dried biscuits with tea, and by evening am able to sit at my armchair at the window and gaze out at the rain that is teeming down on to the rooftops. I take up the *Diario,* which is lying open next to the chair, and begin to read listlessly.

Tuesday evening I felt all weak and I ate a rosemary bread and an omelette and salad and some dried figs.

Wednesday, I fasted.

Thursday evening, an omelette with one egg, and a salad and four ounces of bread altogether.

Friday evening, salad, pea soup and an omelette and five ounces of bread.

Saturday, butter, salad, a rosemary bread, sugar and an omelette.

Sunday the 1st April, I had lunch with Bronzino and I did not eat in the evening.

Monday evening, I had steamed bread with butter, an omelette and two ounces of cake.

Tuesday.

Wednesday.

Thursday.

Friday.

On Saturday I went to the tavern; salad and omelette and cheese. I felt good.

I think I have already read these pages but I'm not sure. It doesn't really matter. Did Pontormo also lose whole days?

So many of my days pass with nothing to say for themselves, when I can't even remember what I have eaten, I can remember no sensations, no thoughts. I presume I must have lived through them but nothing remains to me of them. How little of my life I have actually lived. How little I remember of the books I have read, of the people I have known.

Thursday 20 December

I force myself to get up and go to Modugno's for supper, but the food turns dry in my mouth and I can't swallow it. I leave early. As I do, Ugo's uncle, red-faced and uncertain on his feet, staggers across the square from the bar on the corner where he has been drinking and playing *briscola* since early morning, shouting as he throws down his cards. I see him stagger up the alley, uncertain on his feet. I see him stop and support himself on the wall. I see him fumble with his fly and urinate against the wall then stagger on. I hear the door slam behind him as he enters the house next door. As soon as he is gone I race to my door and lock it behind me. From my room I hear his shouts in the next-door apartment, his wife's voice shrill in reply. I hear bangs and the sound of things smashing, and I hear her scream. I hear his voice roaring over the top of everything. Then silence.

I huddle at my window hardly daring to breathe, feeling his voice penetrate my skull, his animal howls and moans inside me, flames and fire and roaring waters and darkness. Out of it all Ugo arrives at my door.

– *Posso entrare?* he asks. He is breathless and wild-eyed.
– Ugo, you know you mustn't. I told you not to come.
He looks at me imploringly.
– *Mi farà male.*
I feel my resolve begin to waver.

– *Ti prego. Solo per questa volta.*

– Just this time then, I whisper, but never again. Come in, child.

Soundlessly I take him in, soundlessly caress and soothe and clean the wounds.

– Did your uncle do this to you?

He doesn't reply.

I take him into my bed and hold him tight and we lie there clinging to each other like two lost children in the dark. I hear his breath grow quiet and even and shallow and I try to give him a rhythm with my own, slow and calm, as I used to do with my father as a child, to help release him into the arms of sleep, and by doing so I too am caught in its embrace until at last we lie there together, side by side, at peace.

Friday 21 December

School has broken up today for the Christmas break. The children rush out into the streets after the last bell as if they have been trapped for months, as I suppose they have. And I have been the prison keeper.

I need to go to the *Questura,* so I decide to spend a night in Rome and try to get to the queue early before it is too long.

What has happened is difficult to even start putting into words.

I remember catching the ferry over to the mainland. I remember standing on the deck and smelling the damp salty breeze blowing across the water against my face, the oily leaden smell of diesel smoke as the heavy vessel slowed to manoeuvre in the harbour. I remember coming down the gangplank on to the jetty and waiting for a taxi, since the buses were on strike. I remember standing there feeling very conspicuous. I remember a man in a mustard-coloured Cinquecento who stopped and offered me a lift. I remember squeezing into the front seat next to him. I remember the way his lips curled off his teeth as he smiled at me. I remember a joke, his hand slapping my knee, a gesture of friendship. And then the fingers moved and the gesture shifted into something else, the meaning now changed, the hand, the hairy square fingers on my pale knee the same as before when he slapped me in mirth, but the fingers kneading now, moving up, under the edge of my skirt, while I just watched and he looked at me then turned off the main road into a country lane.

I remember lying on my back under the trees and the leaves slowly tumbling through invisible currents, floating, sighing, hovering, golden sunlight and leaves and shade shifting slowly in the gentle autumn breeze – no, not a breeze, no wind at all, yet the leaves still moved, as if of their own accord, perhaps there was a breeze higher up, but here where I lay there was none, the broken chestnut shells from bygone years poking into my back, the soft, loamy earth cushioning my body. When he had done I turned over on to my side and curled up into a ball. There was a faint smell of mushrooms.

Saturday 22 December
Something happened, I am sure. But I don't know what it was. I wish I could remember. It is hovering on the edge of my consciousness, like a dream that I just can't catch hold of. I know that I can't tackle it directly, that is not how dreams work. I will have to wait for it, attentive, pretending to look the other way so as not to frighten it back into hiding.

I get up and put on a pot of coffee and stand waiting in front of the stove while it heats and percolates, enough to distract my mind from pursuing the memory actively, leaving enough space for images to arise. Something brushes through the undergrowth of my thoughts. A mouse? A snake? I clutch at it but it is already gone. I stand rocking gently, there it is again, dry leaves, rustling, rustling, floating down, I am lying on a bed of dried leaves in a forest, in a wood, soft humus under me, warm and fragrant, a scent of green things, growing things, of decay, mould and mushrooms, secret tunnels, aerated underground passages. I lie there abandoned, my clothes loosened, my skirt about my waist, my thighs open. The sun sparkles down through the falling leaves, golden and orange and red. Beside me is a man, lying face down, half across my body, a lover perhaps asleep after sating his passion. I turn my head to look at him and see blood seeping through his clothes down into the soft warm earth beneath us. I see three wounds across his back, puckered and dark, almost black against his navy shirt. I push him off me, his body lifeless, and get to my feet. I see a knife in the grass. I brush the leaves from my clothes and hair and straighten my clothes. I look around. I see a small mustard-coloured Cinquecento on the edge of the clearing.

The coffee is percolating rapidly, noisily, almost a scream. I pour a big mug of coffee and put in lots of sugar. I carry it over to my seat at the window and sit down, wrapping my dressing gown around me for warmth. I take a sip and look out across the rooftops. The big ferry is pulling up the gangplank. It hoots twice and slowly moves away from its moorings leaving a white trail behind it in the water. It will be back in a few hours. It manoeuvres slowly out of the harbour and as it passes the lighthouse at the end of the breakwater, it speeds up. Where is it going? Probably Ventotene, where there is a prison built to resemble Dante's Inferno, with concentric rings leading down to a pit in the centre. What happens in that pit, I wonder.

I sip my coffee. It is ice cold and I become aware that my feet are freezing on the bare tiles and my whole body is tense. I go back to the stove. My eyes fall on the clock above the fridge. It is evening. What have I done all day? I look out of the window. The ferry is just leaving. I see the gangplank being hoisted, hear the hooter blast three times and see the water turn white where the huge propeller churns it as it moves away from the jetty.

Sunday 23 December

Monday 24 December

Tuesday 25 December
Christmas Day.

Wednesday 26 December
My diary has no entries for many days, days of nothing. I
don't remember whether I have been at school, whether I have
eaten or slept or walked out. All around the walls are paintings
I have not seen before. Black. Canvas after canvas of thick
clotted black paint.

Masses of black birds, clotted together in varying degrees of
liquefaction, some putrefied into a seeping mass.

Thursday 27 December
Eggs and salad.

Friday 28 December
I walked to the headland but it was very cold and my head
began to ache so I turned back and came home.

Saturday 29 December

Sunday 30 December
Last night Ugo came again. When I wake up in the morning he
is gone. I wonder for a moment if I have imagined everything,
but then I notice the faint outline of his body on the sheets
beside me and I know that it was true.

I wish Ugo and I could go away somewhere, just the two of
us, far away from prying eyes and hurtful people. We could be
happy by ourselves, I think.

Monday 31 December
New Year's Eve.

Tuesday 1 January

Wednesday 2 January

I go to see a doctor, someone I don't know in the capital, just an anonymous name on a plaque outside an anonymous building. I take a number and sit in the waiting room as one patient after another enters his room and emerges a few minutes later holding a prescription. At last my number is called. Through the doorway I can see *il Dottor* Montalti sitting behind his desk, a large overweight man with a beard, wearing a white doctor's coat that is too tight over his suit. He looks irritable, overworked and depressed. He does not rise when I enter but points to a chair. I sit.

– *Mi dica.*

I hesitate for a moment, and he drops the pen and glares at me irritably.

– *Allora, cos'ha che non va? Si sente male?* So, what's wrong? Are you sick?

There is no way I can even begin to tell him what my fears are. But I force myself to try. I have come so far.

– No, I'm not sick. I think I'm losing my memory. My mind. There are things in my mind that I can't explain and things I can't remember that I am sure I must have done.

He barely registers what I am saying. I see no flicker even of interest in his eyes.

– *Ah. Allora deve andare dallo specialista in malattie nervose. Lo psichiatra.* The psychiatrist. You must go to the psychiatrist.

He punctuates the word carefully, tapping his index finger on his desk to reinforce my memory.

– Psy-chi-a-trist. A specialist in mental illnesses. *Ecco, ti do una lettera.*

He has shifted, imperceptibly, into the familiar form. *Tu.* I no longer deserve the more respectful *Lei.*

He writes, tears off the page and passes it to me. I understand that the appointment is over. I leave the room and walk down the stairs to the street. At the hospital there is another long queue to make an appointment. The first date they can give me is in two months' time. I drop the appointment card in the rubbish bin at the door as I leave. I can't wait that long.

Thursday 3 January

I hear the municipal workers in the street collecting garbage, shouting to each other as they hoist the *cassonetti* up and empty them into the jaws of the garbage truck, mechanical and human sounds disturbing the mid-morning peace. I realise that I am never here at this time of the morning, always at school, always my attention held by the activities of the classroom, the children, oblivious to the sounds coming from the outside, the world where shade and sunlight shift slowly across the houses and bay from hour to hour, subtly transforming them in ways I do not know. It crosses my mind that soon I will always be free in the mornings, and the routine of bells and lessons will no longer punctuate my day. How will I fill my time then? What will give meaning to my existence?

I remember how as a child I also never knew the sounds and smells of the weekday mornings. I never missed a day of school – until my father died. Every year I received a certificate of good attendance.

I look out of my window. It has been raining all morning, and it is now clearing slightly from the west, and beams of light pierce the clouds and shine on the slanting rain where it falls on the sea and disappears. As children we would call this a monkey's wedding; it brings back memories of damp clothes steaming in the sudden unexpected sunlight, warm and wet at the same time. I often used to wonder at the name, wondering whether monkeys really mated or had courtship rituals in these times of confusion. As a child I used to imagine a girl monkey dressed in white posing for a photographer as the rain poured down and sunlight played about her shoulders.

It is difficult to see far, the mainland is shrouded in mist. Only here, nearby, does the play of light on rain relieve the monotony of the greyness, and I know that it will soon close in again to a solid downpour. I feel glad that I have taken the day off and can lie in my bed, dry and comfortable.

Friday 4 January

I have been painting again, but differently now. I am not painting eyes any more. Now I squeeze paint on to the canvas, burnt Sienna and burnt orange as a base, then I cover it over with thick black paint, clotted lumps of it, and with the nail of my forefinger I scratch deep into the blackness, the scratch lines revealing the dark bitter red tones below.

Saturday 5 January

Sunday 6 January

Today is *La Befana*. Epiphany. The end of the holidays. Tomorrow I must go back to school.

I know I have been to the mainland again. I found the torn stub of the ferry ticket in my wastepaper basket yesterday. But I don't remember going there. I am so afraid. I have been watching other people's expressions to see if they notice anything strange about me. I am very careful what I say.

I also found a knife in my handbag, wrapped in wedding gift paper, silver wedding bells on a white background with the words *Tanti Auguri* written over and over again. I unwrap it slowly and draw it from its sheath. The blade is shiny, lethal. I draw it against my thumb, perhaps willing it to be obtuse, but a line of red blood springs up immediately and I stop. It is sharp. I wrap it up again carefully and replace it in my bag.

Monday 7 January

Everything seems to be coming in bits and pieces now. There is no continuity. I spend all my free time in my room, uncertain of what will happen if I go out. I have examined these paintings again and again, but I have absolutely no memory of having painted them. How is that possible? If I didn't, then who did?

A sense of panic rises in me as I try to grasp the meaning

of this. It feels as if everything inside me, everything I know about myself, is unreal. I can't bear to stay here in my room, losing myself in these thoughts. I feel a desperate need to get into my body, to find at least a physical sense of wholeness. I set off up the hill even though it is already late in the day, but I soon come into the mist, thick swirling white sheets of mist that surround and envelop me, cold and wet against my face and hands, and I remember faces and sounds from long ago as if they were with me here now. I see my dog, Manfred, dead years back, come bounding down the path out of the mist, warm brown eyes full of love for me, and I am about to bend and embrace him but he slides away past me and is gone. And I see my mother, firm and young and pretty, laughing at a joke, and then she sweeps past me too and dissolves into nothing.

Tuesday 8 January

I have stopped marking the children's homework. I just can't find the energy any more, now that I know it is all coming to an end.

I feel restless. I need to move, I can't sit still, I walk and walk the full extent of the island, but it is too small, it takes me hours to walk to the end and back and still this feeling of seething restlessness grips me and I set out for another turn. I can take it no longer, and after school on Friday evening I will catch the ferry back to the mainland.

Wednesday 9 January

Signor Cappi tells me that there have been three phone calls from *Ispettore* Lupo at the *Questura* in Rome. He says that *Ispettore* Lupo is expecting me at the *Questura* on Friday. He looks at me quizzically. His face is kind and I wish I could tell him about it all, but there is just too much. I feel strangely indifferent.

Thursday 10 January

Friday 11 January

The policeman at the door to the *Questura* recognises me, I can see from his eyes, but he does not greet me. Perhaps he has orders to be severe, impassive. I tidy my hair and put on some lipstick as I stand and wait for the lift, determined this time to sort things out with *Ispettore* Lupo once and for all. He is in his office sitting at his desk, staring blankly out of the window. I tap on his door. He smiles to see me, but it is not a smile I want to see. I sit down.

He goes straight to the point:

– *È stata indaffarata, vero?* You've been busy. *Allora, si è decisa a dire la verità?*

– You showed me a picture of a woman.

He nods imperceptibly.

– I have been thinking. Yes, I do know her. But what I do with her is my own private business. It has nothing to do with the police.

– *La donna è una, come si dice, una donna di facili costumi.* A woman of easy virtue? *Insomma, una prostituta.* A prostitute.

I don't reply.

His tone changes.

– *Ma cosa fate insieme? Ti piacciono le donne?* What do you do together? Do you like women?

There is an edge of excitement in his voice, which I pretend not to hear. I still say nothing.

– *Mah. Bisognerebbe sentire la Buoncostume. Però c'è un'altra storia qui.* We'll need to speak to the vice squad. But there's something else.

He pulls out the file again, the one I am beginning to know so well. There is the photo of Sabrina again, but there are also two new photos, one of Ugo and one of a mustard-coloured Cinquecento.

I breathe deeply. There is no longer any use hiding.

– I think you need to tell us what you know. What do you know about this man? *Si spieghi.*

– If it is the person I think you are talking about, he gave me a lift a few weeks ago. There was a strike and I couldn't get into town.

– *Il 20 dicembre c'era lo sciopero.* The strike was on the twentieth of December. His body was found on the twenty-first in the woods at Ostia.

– I don't know. I can't remember.

– *Ci deve dire quello che sa.*

His attendant knocks on the door, salutes and addresses *Ispettore* Lupo.

– *Il capo l'aspetta in Direzione.*

He looks at me.

– *Aspetta qui.* Wait here, I'll be back in a minute, he says and goes out.

I grab the folder and race out into the street without thinking.

An icy cold wind is blowing through the streets of the capital tonight, catching up dry leaves and scraps of paper and swirling them around me as I walk. The light from the street lamps is harsh, mercilessly dividing shadow from light. I am the only person out, apart from a solitary prowler creeping by in his car in search of excitement. As he comes abreast of me he slows in anticipation and winds down his window and calls in a low hungry voice, then speeds up when he catches a glimpse of my eyes.

The high-vaulted porticoes near the station are empty. I stand in the shadows invisible to the loiterers driving past in their cars. I wait for about half an hour, hoping that one of the women will arrive, but no one comes.

Either Sabrina has found a client for the night or has decided to stay indoors. I wonder briefly about her home. I imagine a small apartment, a warm kitchen with a pot on the stove, Sabrina in slippers stirring, a television set talking and laughing endlessly to itself. A bright neon light over the kitchen table, a man dozing with his head on his arms, an empty flask of wine in front of him.

I turn my thoughts away from this vision of domesticity as

a lame pigeon flutters up at my feet, startling me, then settles back into the dust in a corner. I wait a few more minutes, reluctant to go to a hotel alone, but at last I begin to feel my toes ache with the cold and I turn back towards the station. It is just beginning to rain and the streets are black and oily, shining lividly in the light from the street lamps traversed by the thin metal tramlines. I leap over a puddle, and as I look up I see a man step out of the shadows for an instant. There is something familiar about him, about the set of his shoulders. It is him. *Ispettore* Lupo. He looks at me in half-mocking recognition. I feel a rush of fear and race away. Shadowy white light, silvery streetlight sparkling on the tramlines, the last few black leaves hanging from the bare branches.

Breathless I let myself in through the small service door in the gateway to the *pensione* and ring the bell. There is no reply at first, but after a few minutes the concierge comes out buttoning his trousers and grumbling at the lateness. He lets me in, takes my document and payment for the night, and makes me sign the register. I feel his eyes on my legs as I wait for the rickety glass lift to arrive in its wrought-iron cage.

I close the door of my room behind me and take off my coat. I am afraid to let my thoughts run anywhere. I wish I had some activity to keep myself busy, to keep my hands busy, my thoughts deadened. I know I am a danger to myself. I pull aside the faded net curtain and peer through the grimy window. I can make out the outlines of a blind service courtyard, covered in pigeon droppings. There is a broken nest on the windowsill with the remains of a dead chick caught up in the dry grass and sticks and bits of rubbish that the bird had chosen to build its nest. I quickly drop the curtain and return to the room. For a while I pace up and down trying to stave off the agitation I feel in my legs and arms, but aware of the absurdity of my movement at last I sit down. I rifle through my bag in the hope of finding something, anything, to distract me. I empty everything on to the chest of drawers. Keys, wallet, lipstick, tranquillisers. I check the bottle. Only four left. Not enough.

Tissues. Penknife. Pen. Notebook. Address book. Ferry ticket. Nothing that will resolve anything. No passport.

The knife. I quickly take it to the window and drop it into the service courtyard. I hear it clatter on the cement below and then all is still once more. I return to the bed.

I pull the folder towards me and open it. Inside are several thinner folders, each containing just a few loose documents. The first is the one that *Ispettore* Lupo has had in his drawer for the past few months. It is divided into two sections – the first contains my personal documents, birth certificate, residence permit, my passport and anagraphical details. The other is thicker and contains the photographs I have seen, the case reports about the *Pensione Arcadia*, the mustard Cinquecento, Sabrina. There doesn't appear to be anything I don't know about. Then there is a folder from the South African authorities – everything they know about me. And then my medical records. This is what I have been dreading.

I open the folder. Brown manila. *Valkenberg Mental Hospital* printed in black across the top. Below, my name and my file number F 56789. Below that again the date of admission and discharge. Then the words *Improved* and *Unimproved*. The second has been ticked.

The room is bare. I clutch my body and hunch over, rocking backwards and forwards and keening under my breath. I lie down fully dressed on the bed and curl up and pull the grimy covers over my head. I can feel my heart thumping in my chest. Agitated: I am agitated tonight. I try to slow down my breathing, to deepen it into my lungs. I am cold and stiff, my shoulders and arms ache with tension as if I have been carrying heavy weights although I have carried nothing heavier all day than my handbag. Gradually my breathing slows. I pull my head free of the covers. Nothing has changed. The room is still here in all its dreariness and squalor. I reach out my hand and switch off the light.

In the dark all the sounds are suddenly amplified. I can hear plumbing gurgling in the walls. I hear a clock ticking somewhere in a room below me. From far off I can hear the siren of an ambulance howl across the empty streets of the city. I follow it in my mind's eye, recognising the streets, the buildings it passes, until I see it turn in at *Regina Coeli* prison. Then silence except for the clock. I hear, down at the bottom of the stairwell, the muffled sound of a door closing. Then footsteps, slow, uncertain on the stairs, the drag of an arm using the wall for guidance. Whoever it is has not switched on the light and is feeling his way up in the dark.

I know it is him.

The footsteps grow closer. Now I can hear him breathing too, slightly out of breath from the two flights of stairs, heavy breath, a big man, not too fit, middle-aged. I search the air for his scent. Nothing, just dust; no, wait, a vague smell of stale sweat, growing stronger now, a metallic smell of city transport, of money changing hands, of hands clutching tram straps, of old cigarette smoke. The sounds stop, he is here, outside, he has discovered my door. I hold my breath. My senses are all ajangle, nerve endings almost painfully alert, overstimulated. I wait. I know he is trying to find me, sniff me out, is waiting to catch a trace of me. Aah, there, he has it. In the dark and silence and airlessness only taste and smell can betray me. My animal scent. I hear him breathe in deeply. I am discovered.

I release my breath. It is no use hiding any longer.

From where I lie, I stretch out my hand, unlock the door of my room and push the door ajar.

I have let it begin. I have turned the key in the lock. Oh dark, dark, dark. Slipping into the infinite confusion of my mind. I lie back again and close my eyes tight. The only sound I can hear is the pounding of the blood in my ears and head. I wait without daring to move. Slowly the pounding subsides.

He moves again, his hand touches the door gently, then grips it, finds it ajar, pulls it open.

I wait for him. The sheets are rough and hard against my cheek. His scent is overwhelming now, filling the room; his breath catches in his throat. He pushes the door shut with his

94

shoulder. He feels his way to the edge of the bed. Now it is just him and me in this tight space, so close I can hardly breathe, yet still I don't move, still I lie and wait.

He sits on the edge of the bed. For a moment he is still, finding his bearings in the dark, he coughs, then coughs again. He turns to me, reaches out his hand and touches my arm. He grunts, then stretches out beside me on the bed, pulls out a packet of cigarettes and puts one between his lips. He breathes heavily. A match flares in the darkness. The flame glints off his pale face then dies and the darkness returns. I catch a glimpse of heavy stubble, wide pores. He inhales deeply, and the air fills with the cloying smell of smoke. He sighs then turns to me.

– *Mi dispiace che sia scappata prima.* I'm sorry you ran out this afternoon. I've been looking for you everywhere.

I can't move. I lie there still, barely breathing. Having opened the door I have spent my last energy.

Wordlessly, with certainty and clarity of movement, he pushes up my cardigan and fumbles and gropes at my chest, then his hands drop, hard, penetrating, the thick hairy fingers pull and push and enter. He withdraws, and lies back on the pillow breathing hard.

– *Ti piacciono le donne, eh*? You like women, eh? *Ti faccio vedere cos'è un vero uomo.* I'll show you what a man can do.

He laughs.

I say nothing.

– *E il bambino*? And the child? You didn't tell me about that.

– *Puttana.*

I hear the sound of a zipper opening, the rustle of clothes and now he is on me, I feel his weight, I feel the loose springs of the bed beneath me, I feel his hardness tearing at me, in me, the rhythmical movement begins again as it has before. I open my eyes.

In the gloom I can see the side of his head beside mine, the large ear, large with hairs sprouting from the centre. There is something about this ear that feels unbearable, that fills me with outrage.

I reach out to the little table beside the bed, unsure of what I am seeking. My hand touches, discards, touches again, at last finds what I am looking for. I run my fingers over its surface, touching, touching, like a tongue touching, touching ever so gently, the bloodied place where a tooth has come out. I brace the muscles of my forearm, then my belly as I test the weight.

Heavy.

I lie, uncertain, in the half-dark, the orange light reflected from the city sky through the grimy window. I turn my head, once more see the side of his head, the fleshy ear, the hairy sprouts, and all my nausea and rage rise in me like bile. My hands feel the heavy marble ashtray, in the dark I lift it. In my mind's eye I hold the door handle with the other hand. He thinks he has me there in that flaccid humid embrace. But I am there, firm, cool-bodied, upright, ready to run.

I pick up the ashtray, I feel the weight in my arm and back and belly. I hold it high above my head and then smash it down on to his head, again and again, like beating a carpet. I feel flesh open wide, fragments of bone separate, embed themselves in the grey flower-like whorls of his brain. He rises, half-rises on his forearms, a prehistoric monster trying to free itself from the mud, the ooze, where its heavy body is trapped. He bellows, then collapses back into suffocation and drowning and death.

But after a while he begins to stir again, and then suddenly he is awake – in the dark I hear him chuckle. Still not dead.

He rolls off me and starts talking, but his thoughts are confused, the speech long and rambling, and I watch the glow of his cigarette in the dark, and sometimes he dozes off in mid-sentence so that I begin to relax but then he starts talking again. And now his speech is slurred so that I can hardly understand what he is saying. At last he falls silent. And when the morning begins to filter into the room he just lies there, inert.

I hear the landlady move in preparation for the day in the rooms below me.

Towards dawn, as the first light fingers its way through the dirty curtains, I get up, wash quickly in the washbasin, straighten my clothes, put the folder into my bag and leave the room, not glancing even once at the bed. I retrieve my identity card from the concierge's desk where it lies in the same place I had left it last night and slip out into the drizzle of the street. The grey light of early morning touches the grey buildings. Someone has strewn breadcrumbs on to the pavement and dirty pigeons peck listlessly at them. Early commuters wait grey-faced at a bus stop, huddled in thick jackets and hats. A few puff raggedly at the first cigarette of the day, anxious to finish it before the bus arrives.

I wait with them, indifferent, transitioning now. I have no umbrella, and my hair grows lank and untidy in the drizzle. At last the bus arrives and I am pushed on board with everyone else. I clasp the strap above my head and allow myself to be rocked gently against the mass of other damp steaming wool-coated bodies packed in around me. I feel a sense of panic at the closeness, as if I can't breathe. I expect the intrusive hand at any minute, I think I am going to faint. At the first stop I manage to push my way to the door, shouting *permesso, permesso,* or it seems to me that I am shouting but all that comes out is a whisper. Surprisingly the human mass parts and I descend on to the street. I find a bench at a bus shelter and sit, feeling lost inside, feeling untouchable, distant, unreal. After a while I get up and walk on, unsettled, and make my way back to the little harbour where the ferries leave for the island.

It is a grey day and drizzling as the *aliscafo* speeds across the smooth waters of the bay. Everything is depressed; even the waves have no energy, just a slow underwater swell, the surface flat and opaque. Drops of water cling to every surface of the boat. I recognise a few of the faces about me but manage to isolate myself behind my book after a few perfunctory greetings. I go straight to school from the port and by nine o'clock I am in class. It is raining here too, a monotonous drizzle. The seagulls have come ashore and are standing along the harbour wall in a row, all facing the same direction. I tell the children to write a composition. The title is 'Rain'. I know I will have to mark it later, or perhaps I won't, but it is better than trying to communicate. I sit at my desk with the register open in front of me, pretending, no, not pretending anything, just sitting.

There are shadows moving in my head and I find it difficult to focus my eyes on the small squares on the pages in front of me. They make no sense; at times they seem intense and dark-coloured, at others they shift far off. I can't quite see the faces of the children either, or remember their names. They look familiar, like the faces of people I have known in my childhood but can no longer place. But I know they are making too much noise and that the principal might come and reprimand us and tell us to keep quiet.

I hold Ugo back at the end of the lesson and, when the other children have left, tell him I need to go away. He looks at me with big eyes.

– *Ma poi torni, vero?*

– Yes, but not for a long time.

– *Ma devi andare subito?*

– Yes, I must leave today.

He hangs his head and rocks from foot to foot.

– *Posso venire con te?*

I can't bear it. My heart leaps. I nod. I tell him to come to my apartment after lunch and to be ready. I tell him not to say a word to anyone.

After school I go back home. It feels strange to open the door of my apartment again, to recognise faint smells I did not even know were there but that belong inseparably to these walls and stairs, smells of mould, of ancient sewers, of the bleach that is used to disinfect the stairs.

My apartment is dry and dusty, and a bitter cold seems to rise from the floor and walls. I wonder if I should light the kerosene heater, but it seems pointless to warm the room if I am going out again at once. The air is stale and cold. I throw open the shutters and a grey light enters the room. I touch the sheets on my bed and they are damp and clammy under my fingers. It feels strange to me, this room, like a place I don't know, even though I have lived between these four walls for the past twenty years. The paintings, the eyes, glare down at me. I go into the bathroom and lift my eyes to the image in the mirror. I do not recognise the face I see there.

I lie down, fully dressed, on my bed. There is not much to do. It is strange that after twenty years I can just walk out and feel no connection to anything. Apart from the paintings. I feel as if I am waiting for something to happen, but nothing does and I can't work out what it would be anyway, and eventually I fall asleep.

Then Ugo comes and I am woken by his gentle tapping on the door.

– *Che facciamo dell'uccellino? Può venire anche lui?*

– The bird can't come with us. We will have to set it free.

We go up the hill together, hand in hand, Ugo carrying the cage. When we reach the grove in the botanical gardens near the cemetery, the most protected spot on the whole island, he puts it carefully on to the ground and opens the cage door. The *cardellino* ignores the open door, perhaps even unaware that another possible world exists outside the bars. Perhaps it has never occurred to the little bird that it could live outside. Perhaps the bars are so much part of its world that it has no concept of sea or sky without the crisscrossing metal lines of the cage that cast shadows across its body, that follow the movements of the sun and moon. I put my hand inside and catch the tiny creature in my fingers. Its body is soft and warm and I can feel its heart beating against my skin. I carefully draw out my hand and bring it to my face, wanting to bless it before it goes, then I pass it to the child. He nuzzles the bird against his cheek for a moment, then, holding my hand tightly, he opens his fingers. It flutters to the ground and sits, bewildered, uncertain what to do. We wait for it to fly away or do something, do anything, but it just crouches there motionless. I bend down and nudge it with my fingers and at last, frightened, it flutters off into the bushes. Ugo sprinkles all the remaining birdseed around on the ground, and then we turn and, still hand in hand, make our way back down the hill to the village.

We go back to my room to prepare for our departure.

We take down all the paintings one by one and make a pile of them on the floor. I put the folders on the top of the pile. Holding Ugo's hand I pick up the petrol can. I tip it, and we smell the oily thinness fill the air. I trail a thread of petrol over the paintings. I look at Ugo. He looks back at me. I pick up the box of matches. There is fear in his eyes but I sense no hesitation. I extract a match and strike it. A little flame flares up, glows blue and gold in the dark. I toss it on to the carpet, and, holding Ugo by the hand, walk down the stairs and out of the door.

The ferry is about to depart. We take our seats in silence and sit, hands crossed, as the engine starts up and the boat pulls out of the harbour. A thin pall of smoke rises from the village, and we turn our heads away and look across the sea to the mainland.

2
Book of Memory

When you are bereft, naked, spiritually or physically, memory can cover you, clothe you, keep you whole. It stops you from shattering, from fragmenting into a million pieces.

Inspired by the words of Ali Bourequat
in the film directed by Ingela Romare, 'On the
Dignity of the Human Soul'

Session 1

He stands to greet her, gestures her towards the chair and sits down across from her. He puts the large, old-fashioned tape recorder on to the table between them and adjusts his position, making himself comfortable. Then he lights a cigarette. She sees the tip glow in the late-afternoon dusk and light up the contours of his nose and mouth, the ancient acne scars on his cheeks. He presses the record button. A thrush chucks in the courtyard outside and rustles in the undergrowth. He looks at her carefully for a moment, then begins:

– *Signorina, Lei sa dov'è, non è vero?* You know where you are, don't you? You know why you are here?

He pauses for effect.

– The accusations are serious. *Le accuse sono grave.* We need to know what happened.

He opens his hands, inviting her to speak.

She doesn't react. She feels nothing. She can see him talking, hear his words, but it is as if he is miles away, in a foreign country, and there is no need for her to respond. She drops her eyes to her lap, watches her finger worrying a loose thread on her jeans. It moves backwards and forwards by itself, flattening the thread one way and then the other, on and on. The room is silent but for the gentle ticking of the clock on the table, the distant roar of traffic.

He waits, watching her carefully.

– *Lo sa perchè è qui, vero?* You know why you are here?

She turns her head and looks out of the window. Her eyes follow the long distorted shadows cast by the setting sun through the foliage, tracing the shadows' outlines, seeking a pattern. She doesn't move. She has made herself impermeable.

– You must talk to me. Why don't you just tell me everything? It would be much easier. I can't help you unless you tell me.

He opens his hands again. She shrugs and gazes up at the darkening sky. She suddenly feels very tired. There's all this big mess of memories. Just a huge jumble. So many things that have happened. She's not even sure whether they happened to her at all. Maybe they happened to someone else, or she saw them in a dream.

– *Deve cercare di parlare*. You must try to talk. You must tell me what happened. Tell me whatever seems important to you, whatever you remember. *Comincia con quello che si ricorda*.

She feels herself slipping back into her mind, the room about her fading into shadow. A picture forms of the park where they used to play as children, the scent of summer and growth, full of big trees and secret places and a pond covered with lotus flowers. But swirling beneath the surface the pond was treacherous, deep with unknown currents.

Her mother warns her: 'Don't go near the water, you might slip and the current will pull you down!'

She wonders what a current is. And suddenly she knows. It is a giant octopus with long tentacles that will grab her and pull her down, down, into the deep darkness. No air, no breath, no life, just a cold watery grave, with her hair and eyes and mouth and throat and stomach all awash.

She hears him sigh, and sees him raise his hand to his face. He inhales and then the tip of his cigarette fragments into glowing sparks as he stubs it out in the ashtray on the table and clears his throat. She looks at him for a moment, hesitating, then her thoughts run on.

There was another pond.

The bed, warm and big and comforting. Her father inviting her in to snuggle and chat on a Sunday morning. Everyone else at Sunday school. Just the two of them there on a sleepy, drowsy morning. Her father never wears pyjamas. He always walks around with the grey hair on his chest bristling and what he calls his 'thing' dangling below his belly. And now cuddled in bed with him, with the morning sun shining through the curtains, dappling light on to the surface of the bed. A strong smell of beer and naked male flesh.

He takes her hand and runs it through the grizzled hair on his chest as he tells her about the war, behind the lines in Libya. She wonders what the lines are. Washing lines? Hopscotch lines? He tells her about the heat in the desert, when his testicles stuck to his leg. Testicles? Tentacles?

And he takes her hand down, so that she can feel where they got stuck. There! And there!

Then he puts her hand on his tentacle and moves it up and down. Is this a current? It feels like a tentacle but he calls it his thing.

– Do you like this, sweetheart?

She feels frozen, unable to say a word.

He answers for her.

– I know you love it. You do, don't you? Answer me!

– Yes, Daddy.

How can she say no? She wants to run away to a safe distance where she can just watch for the ripples and maybe tell her mom if she sees it again.

His hand strays into her pyjamas.

– Why don't you take them off? It's much nicer without them.

She takes them off.

His hand slides down between her thighs. Touching her in those funny places. Pressing, fluttering, smoothing. And his hands pushing and pulling her down under the blankets, into the dark, and then the tentacle catches her and is pulling her down, and she can't breathe and she feels as if she is drowning, all awash, her mouth, her stomach, her hair.

And suddenly it is over, and everyone is home and the Sunday falls back into its usual pattern of Sunday roast with roast potatoes and bullet peas to balance on the back of your fork, and pudding with custard, and then a long ramble in the bush with Mom and the boys. She holds her mother's hand all the way, walking just one step behind her. They call her Mummy's Little Shadow.

The tape recorder stops suddenly. He moves in his seat, then leans forward and switches on a small table lamp; light floods into the dark room. She closes her eyes to adjust, then opens them and looks at him to see what he is thinking. But he seems focused on what he is doing.

Un momento, he says. *Devo cambiare il nastro.*

She waits, glad of the interruption, while he removes the tape from the recorder and replaces it with a new one. She wonders if he is aware that he is recording only himself.

At last he is ready. He raises his eyes and gives her a long searching look, then suddenly notices the time. He gets up.

– *Vedo che è ora. Continueremo domani.* We'll continue tomorrow.

He opens the door and she leaves the room.

Session 2

She enters, takes her seat without looking at him, and closes her eyes. From outside the windows she can hear the sound of traffic and the uneven dripping of rain. A depressed, empty sound.

He clears his throat.

– *Come sta?* I hope you will be able to talk to me today. I am going to put the tape recorder on again. Just in case.

He smiles, a thin-lipped smile that is not reflected in his eyes.

Her mind hears his words but she feels no need to respond. She can't stop her ears from hearing, but she can block her reactions to the words.

– *Vede, Signorina, posso chiamarti Anna, vero? Vedi Anna,* you are in a lot of trouble. You need to help us to help you. *Devi parlare.*

She opens her eyes but doesn't look at him. She is aware of his eyes constantly on her, following her breathing, watching her every reaction, trying to get inside, to penetrate beneath the skin.

– I've been looking at your folder. *La cartella clinica.* Very interesting. I'm interested in your childhood. Your parents, for instance. Your father.

For a moment she stops breathing.

He has noticed her reaction.

Memory floods through her. She is ten. She has come home from school thinking the house will be empty as usual and that she will have to make herself some lunch and then do her homework. She doesn't notice her father's car parked outside under the tree. He has decided on an impulse to take them to the beach.

Why he has decided this she never knows; he hasn't been to the beach with them since she was very small. But this day he is determined. She and her brothers are reluctant to go anywhere with him. He senses this and grows angry.

– Will you bloody kids get into that bloody car at once?

How do you say no? They eventually drag themselves outside to where he stands waiting. What he had wanted to be a happy, fun-filled outing is already turning sour.

As usual his huge black vintage car won't start. He turns the key in the ignition time after time, pressing the starter, but the car just keeps balking at his efforts, refusing to catch. Secretly they begin to hope there will be a reprieve.

– Get out and push!

So they all get out and push the car down the hill with him trying all the time to start it. Suddenly, about a mile down the road, where the road has already turned to a gravel track rough under their bare feet, with proteas high on each side and the smell of buchu strong in their nostrils, the car shudders into life with a roar. He puts his foot on the accelerator to warm up the motor, blasting the wilderness with black smoke and fumes. They all jump in, he turns the car on the track with difficulty, and then roars back into the village and on over the hills covered with young green wheat and then down through the rough coastal scrub to the beach.

It is late afternoon by the time they arrive. A few fishermen stand on the long white beach casting their lines out into the surf. Even though it is the middle of winter and their shadows are tall, the sun is warm on their bare legs and arms. The boys dive into the icy water and swim briskly for a few minutes, then come out puffing and covered in goosebumps. The light catches the drops of water in their hair and lights up their faces like haloes. They run up and down the beach to get dry. They start quarrelling as usual, their aggression and frustration more easily unleashed on each other.

He stays near the car, taking slugs from a plain medicine bottle filled with a transparent liquid. After a while he sets off, rather unsteadily now, towards the water's edge, where he has noticed some fishermen pulling in a catch.

– What did you get? he asks them, slurring slightly.

– *Dis 'n haai*. They point at the rough grey shark still struggling on the sand.

– Hey, kids, come here. Come and look at this.

Their hearts drop but they go and look. They know it is best not to defy him in public.

– Wouldn't it be bloody funny to have a shark in our fish pond, hey? Let's take it home. Can you imagine what the cat will do when it tries to drink and sees a fin coming towards it in the water? It'll be bloody funny.

They are embarrassed, humiliated at being part of him, of his absurd ideas, of his slurred speech. His shame is their shame. They wish they could disappear.

She opens her eyes and sees him watching her carefully. He looks frustrated, bored. She closes her eyes and lets her thoughts slip back to the past.

Her father negotiates a price and they lug the still squirming creature back to the car. By this time he is staggering slightly.

– Who wants to drive? He points at her fourteen-year-old brother. – You drive.

David is small for his age and can barely see over the dashboard or reach the pedals with his feet. From where she stands outside the car, it looks as if no one is driving.

Even as she remembers this, she feels her stomach turning. She pulls the cushion out from behind her back and snuggles it against her body. But the memory keeps coming.

They all pile in, their father in the back. He is drinking steadily and openly now, and is barely coherent. No one says a word. It is growing dark quickly, and her legs have turned mottled with the cold. Blue and pink and white. Sand scratches her thighs where they rub against the leather seat. She feels a tight bitter anger in her chest.

Sitting as tall as he can, David drives slowly down between the dunes and along the shady avenue of bluegum trees. The cold dusty scent of eucalyptus fills the car. He doesn't notice the police car parked by the side of the road in the long shadow of the trees. Only when he hears the siren behind him does he turn his head and see the policeman signalling him to stop.

– Dad, it's the cops!

– Oh Christ! Quick, hide the liquor!

They push the brown medicine bottles under the seat and sit paralysed, waiting. An overweight policeman saunters up to the door of the car.

– License please, *lisensie asseblief.*

Her father opens the door on the far side, trips and falls out on to the ground. He pushes himself to his knees and then unsteadily to his feet. He holds on to the door of the car for balance.

– Listen here, officer, my son's just having a driving lesson.

The policeman studies him, and then inspects each of the children in turn. No one says a word.

– *Meneer*, you are drunk. Come with me. Don't you kids move!

They sit in the dark vehicle and wait. They isolate themselves within themselves and don't see their father being led away. After what seems like a very long time of cold and dark, the policeman returns and points at David.

– You, *seuntjie*, come with me.

A different policeman gets into the car without saying a word and drives the two remaining children over the dark hills to home. The car pulls up at last outside the house and they slip out while the policeman speaks to their mother in a low serious voice.

As on so many other occasions, she doesn't know what the

outcome of this episode was. It is blanked out in her memory.

It is now almost completely dark in the room. She breathes deeply, flicks an invisible spot of dust off her jeans.

He sits forward and looks at the small clock on the table beside her.

– *È quasi ora. Dobbiamo finire. Ma riprenderemo domani.* I'll see you tomorrow.

He stands and shows her to the door.

Session 3

He opens the door and gestures her to her seat. She sits down. She glances at his face and he looks back expectantly. She closes her eyes to keep him out. Her thoughts are swirling about, dark wings fluttering through her brain, confusing her. She looks down at her lap. Her finger reaches out towards the loose thread and begins to work it backwards and forwards. Slowly her thoughts settle. Where was she yesterday?

Her father.

When she first has the idea of killing her father. How the idea begins to flit in and out of her mind and won't go away.

It is a rainy winter's night. About seven o'clock. Warm yellow light spilling out on to the wet lawn through the window. She is playing in her secret place behind the couch. She is surrounded by the smell of cooking. Onions frying. Her mother is making braised steak and mashed potatoes and gem squash and green beans for supper. She knows she is going to gag on the beans as usual. Jelly and custard for afterwards. The radio, a big brown wooden box with black dials, is transmitting Mark Saxon and Sergei Gromyko in *No Place to Hide*. Her father is in his big chair next to the fireplace. Still wearing his white hospital coat with CPA/KPA stamped in red across the breast in a cross intersecting at the P. A glass of beer on the armrest. A crate of beer half hidden behind his chair. There is the smell of beer mixed with the smell of onions. He begins to quarrel with her brother, then leaves the room, but returns almost immediately and pulls something out of his pocket. Small, metallic. She thinks, *That's a gun*. It doesn't look real or dangerous, but she knows without question that it is. From where she sits she can see the black hole leading inwards to emptiness. She crouches down as low as she can to get out of sight of the hole. Things move fast. There is screaming and shouting and running feet and cold and dark and then she is in the car with her mother and the boys and they are driving away fast. No time for feelings, just the need to get away.

They park under a jacaranda tree outside the police station. Nobody says a word. The blue flowers are heavy with water. The rain drips down on to the metalwork chassis of the car making loud plonking sounds, or flatly and dully on to the tarmac outside. They are too proud to go inside and ask for help, so they just sit there and wait. The night passes slowly. Her legs and feet turn numb with the cold.

She stops in mid-memory, bothered by a detail. If it was winter there wouldn't have been flowers on the jacaranda tree. They flower in November. But it was winter, of that she is sure. She remembers how cold it was.

At some point, after many hours, they go back home. They park in the street in front of the house. Her mother and the boys discuss what to do next. She is too little, they don't ask her opinion. They decide at last to go into the house and see where he is. They decide that Anna should go in front because she is his favourite and he is least likely to hurt her. At least, she thinks that is the reason. She is terrified, but also feels quite special and important.

The house is dark, the garden is dark, it is raining so there are no stars or moon to light the way. They climb through the fence and walk across the black wet lawn, she in her shorty pyjamas, her bare feet icy cold and wet. What will they find? Will he be waiting behind the door in the dark, shadowy, mad, ready to kill? Will he have shot himself and be lying on the ground in a puddle of blood? Her childish imagination runs riot. But she forces herself to keep walking. They reach the front door and hesitate, then push her forward. She stands on tiptoe to turn the door handle.

The memory ends here. She doesn't know what happened next. She can't remember. There's a kind of dead end. It all goes blank. She knows that she went to school as usual the next day; she always did. She knows that it was never mentioned again. She doesn't know how it ended. Perhaps he had gone to bed.

A few days later when she comes home from school she sees him swaying in the doorway at the top of the stairs that lead down into the garden, his heavy body outlined against the afternoon sun. It is a question of an instant. She doesn't even think.

He doesn't hear her coming up behind him. She reaches up. Her hand touches the worn fabric of his white hospital jacket, feels the warmth of his body beneath. A quick push is all it takes. There is no resistance.

He tumbles down head first, slowly, as she stands there where he had stood only a second before, her hand on the doorframe, watching. His body is soft, offering no resistance, like a lifeless object. And when he reaches the bottom he lies there motionless.

She goes to her bedroom and lies down on her bed in her school uniform. She falls asleep. When she wakes up her mother is home. She can hear her moving around the kitchen. Her mother tells her there has been an accident and her dad has been hurt.

He isn't dead. It's actually quite difficult to kill someone, she realises: the body puts up a huge fight for survival. Her mother calls the doctor who brings him around and helps him to bed. He seems fine and the doctor leaves. They all go to bed.

Her father begins talking, long rambling monologues the way he often did when he was drunk. And her mother can't sleep because of his talking, on and on. She is worried because she has to go out of town on an audit tomorrow, she must get a good night's sleep. At last she comes to Anna's bed and asks if she can change places with her. Will Anna sleep in her bed?

How high her mother's bed seems that night. She climbs it like a mountain. She lies in the dark room beside him hoping he won't notice her. But he does. In the dark she hears him chuckle. He stretches out his arm and pulls her to him and she goes.

And when it is over, she lies praying for death for him. Perhaps for herself as well.

But he is awake beside her in the bed. In the dark. He lights another cigarette. She hears the clink of glass as he pours more beer, the sound of him swallowing. And then the talking starts again, about work, about Van his assistant, and all the usual things, and her eyes grow heavy. But something is different tonight, not quite the same; his thoughts are confused, the speech long and rambling more than usual, and she watches the glow of his cigarette in the dark, and sometimes he dozes off in mid-sentence but just when she is beginning to relax he starts talking again. And now his speech is slurred so that she can hardly understand what he is saying. At last he falls silent.

As the morning begins to filter into the smoky, beery room, her mother bustles in to start the day. But he just lies there, inert. And then her mother is on the phone to the doctor and the children are packed off to school.

She remembers the scratchy angriness she felt as dawn fingered its way through the curtains into the dank-smelling untidy room where he lay unconscious, silent, his breathing now shallow and slow.

Early, much earlier than usual, she is up and pulling on her school uniform, the light-blue shirt and tie, the navy tunic, the navy blazer over the top. Underneath, the thick cotton bloomers and grey socks. It is cold and drizzling as she makes her way up the hill to school. She is the first child in the playground and she doesn't know what to do. The school buildings are still locked. She goes and sits on the dead tree trunk in the glade and waits. Blankly, thoughtlessly, comatose like her father.

There is no one at home when she comes back from school. The house is quiet and cold. There is nothing to eat but she isn't hungry. She goes outside and the chickens flock to the fence of their run. They've obviously not been fed. She goes back to the kitchen and measures out a bowlful of food and takes it to them. They fight over the corn that she sprinkles about.

She crouches down and holds out a few kernels on the palm of her hand to her favourite hen – a scruffy, skinny, henpecked creature with a torn comb and bare neck who has managed to avoid the pot for so long because she looks so unhealthy. The hen turns her head to one side, glares at Anna with a beady eye and at last pecks the grain from her hand, then jumps back. Now that Anna has nothing for her the hen ignores her. She starts to sing a hymn from Sunday school that she feels sure the hen must like, 'Under His Wing', but the bird takes no notice and keeps scratching around in the dirt. The rooster takes a few cautious strides towards her, but when he sees that her hands are empty he moves away. She is glad. He scares her.

Her mother comes back after dark. She is tired and looks worried. There is no supper, but no one is hungry. They sit in the lounge and she tells them that their dad is in hospital. He is in a coma. There has been massive haemorrhaging in his brain from the fall. He is on a life-support system.

Everything seems flat, unemotional. Drained of meaning. Even now she can't feel anything.

They sit and wait. At about ten the phone rings. It is the doctor. The damage is too extensive. The hospital needs permission to disconnect the life-support system. There is nothing the family can do but wait for him to die.

They wait. She prays for him to die.

At two am the doctor calls to say he is dead. Wordlessly, without looking at each other, they get up and go to bed. Does she sleep? She doesn't know. She supposes so.

In the silence, she hears him light a cigarette, hears him take a deep draw and then blow the smoke out in her direction. She feels it curl its tendrils about her, creeping under her clothes and into her hair.

The next morning she goes to school as usual. In the playground she tells her friends she has a secret, feeling strangely proud and special. But she won't tell them what it is. The bell goes for school and they file into class. They stand for the Lord's Prayer.

– *Our Father, who art in Heaven.*

She bursts into wild, uncontrollable tears. The teacher takes her to the sick room. She makes her lie down on the narrow bed in the corner of the room and covers her with a blanket. She asks Anna what is wrong. She remembers saying:

– My father died last night.

The teacher pats her shoulder, blankly. She quite clearly doesn't know what to do, whether to go back to her classroom, stay here with Anna or go to the headmaster. She is young, fresh from teacher training college, inexperienced. Eventually she leaves Anna alone.

The child lies there in the bare room. She doesn't know what to do. She doesn't feel sick. There is no reason for her to be in bed. She doesn't want to be alone. After a few minutes she gets up, straightens the bed and goes back to class. Everyone avoids looking at her as she walks in, although she can feel their eyes on her back when she sits down. She knows the teacher must have told them.

It suddenly occurs to her that they don't know that she has murdered her father. Because that is what she suddenly realises she has done.

– I'm a murderer, she thinks to herself with a sense of utter isolation and bereavement.

For days the rest of the world falls into shadow for her. Only his death is real, highlighted by her mind. She waits in an agony of terror and excitement for the police to come and arrest her. She feels quite sure they will put her into jail and sentence her to the electric chair.

A few days later she comes home from school and the house is full of people and flowers. She has never seen so many people in the house before. They've never had visitors before. It is a cold, overcast, rainy day; the smell of lilies and chrysanthemums and mud is overwhelming. The smell of the dead.

She can hardly breathe. She tries to reach her mother but there are too many people in the way.

– Not now, Anna, she says.

There are scones and teacups and plates laid out in the lounge but no one is eating yet. She ducks under the table and sits as far as she can from the sea of tweed jackets and damp woollen skirts and heavy shoes. It is dark and cool and quiet in there. She curls up tight hoping that no one will notice her. But then the tablecloth is lifted and a huge face distorted by gravity appears, wet lips outstretched for a kiss. She withdraws and turns her head, and the lips pull apart to show teeth. She is dragged out and forced to submit to the kiss.

A cousin takes her to a car and they set off for a drive that keeps them away all afternoon because it is not thought right for children to go to funerals. They go to Bainskloof and Wemmershoek Dam, and Steenbras Dam, which looks like pictures she has seen of Canada. Perhaps they are in Canada. She wishes she could go far away to Canada where no one can find her. She doesn't know her cousin who is much older than her, and they don't talk at all. Just drive, silently, in the grey drizzle. They get home after five. Everyone has gone; the house is empty, only the flowers remain to remind them that anything out of the ordinary has happened. But she doesn't dare to ask about it. She imagines *the funeral* has taken place although she doesn't know what a funeral would look like. She wonders if her father has been buried in the graveyard that she and her mother and brothers walk past every Friday evening on their way to the library, where the owls hoot in the trees.

A few days later she helps her mother to clear out his cupboards. They put everything into cardboard boxes. They never speak of him again.

There is an autopsy and the official version is that he had been drinking as usual, he had fallen down the stairs and hit his head on the floor and lost consciousness. No one suspects her part in it. She is the only one who knows what really happened.

In those months after the funeral she is always at home. The house feels dark and cold but she has no desire to be anywhere else. There is no need to go and play at her friends' any more or to go and sing to the chickens. In fact she has no desire for company. The only thing she craves is food. Sweet, sugary, milky things, comforting and soothing. Every day when she comes home from school, alone in the dark, cold house, she bakes herself batches of scones, or cakes, which she eats by herself in the darkened lounge. She takes no pleasure in it.

Session 4

She enters and sits down in the usual seat. She looks at him quickly from under her brows, then averts her head. She had almost been looking forward to coming here today. To continuing her thoughts. But now that she is here she feels tired.

He smiles and sits down opposite her.

– *Allora, Anna, non ti sei ancora stancata di questa storia?* Aren't you tired of this story yet? All you need to do is talk. *Tutto qui.* That's all we need.

She feels so tired. She wishes they would just let her be. She doesn't want to sit here in this room with this man watching her, pushing her to think and remember and feel.

She closes her eyes and slips back into the past.

She is twelve when she first meets Luke. She has just come home from boarding school for the holidays. He is her cousin from out of town, about ten years older than her, who has come to stay with them while he is studying at the university. She has never met him before.

She walks into the lounge and there he is, deep in conversation with her mother. He is watching himself in a mirror as he talks, his eyes only on himself. He doesn't notice her standing in the doorway and carries on talking. She feels like an intruder and goes back to her room.

She remembers that first meeting vividly, his heavy straight hair, his huge brown eyes, his quick movements. She realises it must only have been much later that she noticed his fine wrists and ankles, the delicate hands, the square well-manicured fingernails, although they all seemed to be present in her mind in that first moment. She remembers his mocking gravelly voice, the histrionics, the swagger.

The impact on her is massive; she can't get him out of her mind.

Luke is always so busy that she hardly sees him. She hears his car skid into the driveway in the early hours of the morning, feels the slam of the front door shake the floorboards under her bed, and his footsteps run to his room. But one day, he knocks on her bedroom door to say hello. He raises his eyebrows sarcastically at the music she is listening to on the radio. A few minutes later he brings her an LP of Bruno Walter conducting the Berlin Symphony Orchestra playing Beethoven's Sixth Symphony, the *Pastorale*.

When she comes back for the next holidays, he offers to take charge of her sentimental education. Music, literature, philosophy, politics. He starts by bringing her a copy of *The Catcher in the Rye*. She is intrigued by the silver cover of the paperback, how special it feels. She devours the book in the space of a few hours, but then she doesn't know what to do with it. She wants to give it back to him and say something witty, something that will make him think she is grown-up and sophisticated. But she can't think of anything to say. Eventually she leaves it on his bed while he is out.

For a few days he ignores her. She is grateful for his silence.

Then one evening, on his way out, he taps on the door. He holds out a new book. And a recording of Rachmaninov's Piano Concerto No 2.

– I think you might find these interesting.

The book is *The Second Sex*, by Simone de Beauvoir. She blushes and quickly slips it under her pillow, embarrassed to have that word between them. After dinner she goes straight to her room to read, but this time she is disappointed. There is

118

little about sex and no story at all. She forces herself to read it to the end, and puts it back on his bed. She is still twelve years old.

A week later he is back with another book, this time by Masters and Johnson. He gazes at her intently as he hands it over. *Human Sexual Response*. And it is all she wants to know and more. He begins to fill her imagination in the long dreary days when she is away at boarding school. She begins to dream of him at night in her narrow convent bed.

And then come the banned books, Marx, de Sade, Achebe, books she is vaguely aware she could be arrested for having. She remembers one in particular about the distribution of land in South Africa and the Group Areas Act. The books take her out of and above the conventionality of her family, the blinkered mysticism of the nuns, the giggling awkwardness of the other girls at school. She remembers telling her friends that she has become a communist.

One night she climbs into his bed. And the next night he follows her back to hers. The encounter is quick and shameful. They do not speak and it is all over in minutes.

Then one day when she comes back from school for the holidays he is there with a wife. Anna sits in her school uniform watching them from the window of her upstairs room as they lounge in the garden, next to the statue of Mercury, drinking tea and eating scones. She hears the woman's husky laughter as he takes her bare foot into his lap and holds it between his hands, massaging it, circling the instep with his thumb, softly, tickling, and then slips his hand up her calf and under her dress.

He takes his wife's hand and leads her inside. Anna knows exactly what they are going to do. She can hardly breathe. But later that night when the whole house is asleep he comes to her bed. Furtive and silent and shameful.

From one day to the next she stops talking. Words become impossible, and language a foreign land. Dangerous, incomprehensible, treacherous.

She knows that if someone were to threaten her life, or if the building were to catch fire, some part of her would be able to react, would cry out, would run. She knows it is not a physical barrier. Somewhere, some part of her knows she could choose to be different, to break the silence and paralysis. Except she chooses not to.

She thinks a minute. Perhaps not. Perhaps she had no choice. Perhaps she was too young. Perhaps she was still caught in the web of events that had rendered her mute.

For a long time nobody notices. You can get by on nods and shakes of the head and smiles, she thinks. Especially smiles. People love to talk about themselves, and if you smile they think you agree.

She smiles often.

She can of course still understand. And thoughts still course through her brain using words. It isn't that she has lost the ability. It is just that language as communication has become impossible, too painful, too dangerous.

He shifts in his chair, lights a cigarette and inhales deeply. She has almost forgotten that he is there.

They ask her what is wrong. Explain. Be responsible. Account for yourself. But she can't. She doesn't know. There are some things she can't tell them about but also that she can't work out, can't make the connections in all the mess of memories – which events caused this to happen. She just knows that she feels unsafe and ashamed, so she withdraws to a place deep inside herself. She walks the streets and makes eye contact with strangers, staring at them until they avert their eyes.

Her mother makes an appointment for her to see a doctor.

She sits, fifteen or sixteen years old, hunched up on a low armchair in the waiting room, head bowed, oblivious to everything around her. The glass coffee table piled high with magazines holds no attraction. She is dressed in her school uniform – thick beige stockings, heavy brown lace-up shoes, blue dress, blue blazer, anonymous. Her long brown hair hangs loosely about her face, in defiance of school regulations, like a screen.

At last the receptionist signals to her to go inside. The doctor sits across a high desk clear of everything except an empty brown file and a pen. She looks down at her hands. He has a rich Persian carpet spread across the floor of his consulting room. His shiny black shoes surmounted by grey-and-black pinstriped trousers rest amongst its scarlet-and-blue peacocks and swirling flowers.

– So, Anna, tell me about yourself.

She doesn't know what to say. What can she tell him? What is there to say? So she sits there as the doctor speaks, hearing but not really hearing what he is saying. He examines her reflexes, taps her knee with a little hammer making her jerk. Asks her questions that she doesn't answer. He gives up eventually. He gets up and calls her mother into the room. Anna watches them talking, watches the smiles, the mouths opening and closing. Back in the car, a short journey to Volkshospitaal in Gardens, to another doctor, nurses, being clothed in a surgical gown and told to get into bed. Lying waiting. No, not waiting. Just lying. Not sick. Not anything.

The hospital is small, more like a sprawling Victorian house, her room large, with elaborate pressed ceilings and a bay window looking out on to the park with Table Mountain rising above the trees behind it. She lies there wordlessly, not caring about anything.

The next morning she is placed on a stretcher and wheeled into an operating theatre. The doctor from the day before, an anaesthetist, two nurses. They apply an electrode to each of her temples, others to her chest. The electrodes on her temples are attached to a little metal box, strangely primitive in appearance, like an old-fashioned, enamel-coated butcher's scale. Two dials. A switch.

The anaesthetist traffics around her arm, finds an artery. The doctors exchange glances. The anaesthetist tells her to count to ten. She remembers counting to seven before the synthetic surge floods her nostrils and brain.

He uncrosses and crosses his legs, glances surreptitiously at the clock.

When she wakes up her head and neck ache. It hurts to open her eyes. She is back in her bed. She is aware of a flash through her brain, like having looked straight into the sun, except it won't go away. Everything is white. Walls, ceiling, pressed ceiling with little plaster flowers around the edges, sheets, blankets. She tries to cling to details and patterns but nothing will stay in her mind. The nurses are white. The food is white. Mashed potatoes, steamed chicken, cauliflower, ice cream. There is nothing else. No thoughts, no inner dialogue. She sleeps. She wakes up and finds one of the electrodes still on her chest. The nurse tells her to leave it there. They will use it again.

Every second day the treatment is repeated. She forgets how often. Some days she manages to count to eight before the surge fills her brain. Other days she only gets to five. At some point it all becomes confused. Just flash after flash of blinding light. She doesn't remember leaving the hospital.

She sighs.

Language, she thinks, can't really express what happened. She remembers how all her thoughts slowed down. Disappeared. Just blinding whiteness and pain and confusion. Perhaps that is the point of the treatment. It feels like the punishment she has been expecting for so many years.

Her mother visits and brings her chocolate. White chocolate. She is hungry, starving, and devours slab after slab, larva-like. One day, she supposes, her mother comes to fetch her. She has been in hospital for a month. About twenty shocks through her brain. Give or take a few. There are no records. All the old records have been destroyed, along with many memories of those years.

There are more doctors. A few weeks later, somehow, she doesn't remember how, she ends up in the state psychiatric hospital that lies on the narrow finger of land between two rivers.

Sometimes she thinks she has never left the hospital. Perhaps she never will. Perhaps all these years since have simply been a dream. Perhaps she sits on a bench in the sun, an old woman on a back ward, dreaming her life away, conjuring up islands and emperors and oceans and ruins while a nurse in white watches silently on.

At night she lies in her narrow metal bed watching the lights from a passing car shine through the barred windows of the dormitory and cast moving shadows on to the opposite wall. Then the car rounds the bend near the river and disappears into the city of light, and the room falls back into darkness and she is once more alone with her thoughts. She listens to the heavy breathing of the other women who lie trapped in drugged sleep or cry out in terror from the deep places of their nightmares.

A bed, a small low cupboard where she keeps her toothbrush and paints; the sum total of her world.

Sometimes in the morning, after a greasy breakfast of eggs and toast and coffee, she stands at the fence of the exercise yard, her fingers caught in the diamond mesh wire, and watches the birds down at the water's edge where they eat and breed and squabble and die. One day she saw a pelican. It flew up from the river towards her, heavy-bodied, deep-chested, its wings flapping powerfully to free itself from the earth's pull; it passed within arm's reach, so close she could hear its heart beat. She swears she heard its heart beat.

Three months later she is discharged against medical advice. *Unimproved.* The doctor tells her they can do nothing for her if she won't speak. And that she has read too much Eliot and Sartre. She begins to wonder about psychiatrists.

For a few months after being discharged she stays in a furnished room near the university to prepare for her school-leaving exams, which she had missed while she was in hospital. The only person she sees in those months is Luke, her cousin, who arrives unannounced outside her window, heaves himself up and drops on to her bed. It is only a question of a few minutes. He takes her there, where she lies, in silence, and then straightens his clothes and climbs back out of the window.

As soon as the exams are done, she is driven to the airport and put on board an Alitalia flight via Kinshasa to Italy. Her mother has met someone who knew someone who had studied Italian at the University for Foreigners in Siena and had lots of fun. Not knowing what else to do with Anna, she puts her on a plane and sends her to Italy for a year to study Italian.

He glances at the clock. She sighs.

Yes, she knows, time to go.

Session 5

She sits down in her usual place. She feels anxious and afraid. What can he be thinking, why does he keep bringing her back here day after day if she will not talk to him, will not tell him anything? What will they do to her if she can't speak?

He lights a cigarette and clears his throat.

– *Mi è venuta un'idea*. I've been thinking. Would you like to try to lie on the couch and see if that works better? You might feel more relaxed.

He points at a chaise longue against the wall, which she had not noticed before. She looks at it, uncertain what to do.

– Why don't you give it a try? If you don't like it you can always go back to the chair.

She gets up reluctantly and takes a few steps to the chaise. She sits down on the edge of it and looks up.

He is staring at her. She can see the curiosity in his eyes, senses his excitement.

She feels the breath catch in her throat. She doesn't know how to say no, but this feels impossibly dangerous, terrifying. She feels as if she is going to faint. But there seems to be no other option, no alternative. At last she forces herself to breathe deeply, and stretches out on the couch.

Unable to stop herself, she turns over and begins to weep. She can't stop. She cries for the whole hour.

Session 6

She comes into the room and goes straight to the chair, ignoring the couch. She sits back and closes her eyes, refusing to engage. The memories begin at once. Strange flat emotionless memories, but very clear.

She remembers staring out of the window as the airplane lands in Rome and taxies towards its terminus buildings. End of the line. It is a cold day at the end of February. She is seventeen. She is mute. She is completely alone.

Her mother has arranged for her to spend a week in Rome sightseeing before she catches the bus to Siena. She is booked into the *Pensione Arcadia* near the Villa Borghese gardens. Outside the airport is an empty taxi rank. She feels silly and conspicuous, standing there with her suitcase next to her, waiting. A man, leaning against a wall, grins.

– *Ci ha d'aspettà. Fino alle cinque non passano più.*

Anna looks at him without understanding.

– Ah, *straniera*! No taxi. *Taxi sciopero.* After five o'clock, maybe. *Capisci?* Strike.

He comes closer.

– Where you going? he asks.

She pulls out the address and shows him.

– Come. I take you.

She tries to think of what she should do but if there is a strike there doesn't seem to be any alternative, so she nods, yes.

He loads her large Samsonite suitcase on to the back seat of the tiny mustard-coloured Cinquecento, since it will not fit into the boot, and then they squeeze themselves into the front. He speeds out of the *piazzale* and on to a country road flanked by huge advertising placards. She eyes her companion. He grins back and changes into a lower gear. Then casually, as if it were the most natural thing in the world, his hand slides off the gear lever and on to her knee. And still he grins. She looks at the hand, square, strong, with tufts of hair growing from the fleshy parts. Fingernails cut short but not too clean. As she looks, the hand begins to move, to knead and squeeze her flesh. Then it

125

shifts upwards and inwards. He looks at her quickly, sees no opposition, and turns the car off the road into an abandoned lot. He parks amongst the nettles next to a graffiti-covered wall, and unbuttons his fly. He puts his hand on her neck and pushes her face down.

He drops her off a few hours later in front of the *Pensione Arcadia*. She checks in, trying to hide the abrasions on her lips and face from the curious eyes of the manager who accompanies her to her room, eyeing her legs as she walks.

For a few days the hotel becomes her home, while she waits for the week's holiday to come to an end. Like home, it is not a safe place, and so it feels familiar. She doesn't unpack her suitcase, knowing that soon she will be moving on.

Each time she comes back, he is there waiting for her, the hotel manager, and he accompanies her to her room. He has taken to coming inside, using his skeleton key, after checking that no one, especially not his wife, is looking. He tells her to wash herself first in the bidet. It is a quick, silent business, over in a few minutes with only a minimal disturbance of clothing, and then he is gone. She lies on the bed where he leaves her, curled up with her eyes closed.

But every morning she feels obliged to get up and pretend to exist. Like when she was a child and got up to go to school every day, no matter what had happened in the night. When she emerges on to the street the man in the mustard-coloured Cinquecento is always waiting for her outside the door. They don't return to the abandoned lot. Once they go to the woods and lie on the damp ground, and the sun shines through the floating golden chestnut leaves as they fall silently to earth. Another time he takes her to a tiny flat, which she understands he has borrowed from a friend. Sometimes he brings a friend. Sometimes two. He allows them to take part. She goes where he takes her. Without saying a word. And in the afternoon she comes back to the ministrations of the manager.

If his wife is there, he takes Anna out for a drive. One day they sit in the car beneath the stands of the Teatro Olimpico along the banks of the Tiber, just past the Ministero degli Esteri. His beard is rough under the rough cement arches; it tears the skin around her mouth. On the last day she realises she is bleeding, her mouth is swollen and bruised, it hurts to walk. The man in the Cinquecento takes her to the bus stop and leaves her there next to her suitcase. She has not eaten for a week. She has been too afraid and ashamed to go into a shop or restaurant and order food.

The bus takes three hours to reach its destination, climbing higher and higher into the Apennines. It begins to snow, covering everything with a soft veil of white. It is dark by the time the bus pulls in to the main square and stops. She alights with the other passengers and stands waiting beside the bus to collect her suitcase. And then she faints in the snow.

She has reached her limit.

A shopkeeper carries her into his shop, which sells ecclesiastical accoutrements. She comes back to consciousness reflected in a thousand glittering surfaces, surrounded by statues of saints and golden crucifixes and vestments and habits for priests and nuns. The owner calls a taxi, and she is taken to Signora Bruna's.

Session 7

She stands at the door, reluctant to come inside. He waits. At last she sits down and stares out of the window. When he sees her eyes return to the room, he asks:

– *Cosa stai pensando*? Where are you today?

For some reason she can't help smiling. She tries to stop herself but her face keeps twisting into a smile. He notices and smiles back.

– Something feels different today? *Me ne vuoi parlare?*

She looks at him, then shakes her head. She sighs and closes her eyes.

In Siena, she doesn't study Italian. How could she study Italian? She can't speak any language.

Slowly, after many months, she doesn't remember how, she

finds her way to the *Accademia di Belle Arti*, the university art school, housed in a thirteenth-century Franciscan convent with high vaulted windows looking out over the hills to infinity. And there, silently, she begins to make shapes in clay. At first she destroys everything she makes. Then she begins to shape a woman's head. Day after day she goes and works on it, moulding and pressing it until the professor tells her it is done. She should cast it in bronze.

She thinks back. Such good work, the slow remaking of a life. She begins to talk to him, a few halting words in Italian. *Grazie. Come faccio? Grazie*, speaking of grace. Then more. Slowly she learns to speak again. The new words, the Italian words, feel clean. Golden. Usable. Safe. Like the brimming over of a golden liquid. She rejoices in this new language, in its wonderful crisp sounds the meaning of which still often evades her. *Cinquecento-cinquanta-cinque. Terontola. Castruccio Castracane.*

She never learns it formally, as a comparison to another language, finding parallels in grammar and meaning. No. It is something separate. She learns it in the street, as it were; pointing to something she is told its name and that becomes it. *Mela* has no connection to the word *apple* and all its implications. It is just a fruit. And it tastes and smells of *mela*. Her two worlds are separate. Even today she finds it almost impossible to translate from English to Italian and vice versa.

Slowly she learns to seek out the other, or at least not to withdraw, like a sea anemone, at the touch of a hand. Dust. Clay. Mud. Remaking herself.

One day she walks out and the grass is green. Green, so startlingly green and beautiful it makes her gasp. She didn't know there was so much beauty in the world. It is just a scruffy patch of grass on the side of a road, edging out from dirty melting snow, but she remembers it as one of the most important turning points of her life.

Life feels infinitely interesting now. She decides she wants to understand things. She registers for a long-distance degree in

Anthropology and Psychology through the University of South Africa and studies Arabic and Zulu as part of the course.

At the same time she applies to study Philosophy at the University of Bologna and is accepted on condition that she pass a language test in Italian first. She passes the test, to her great joy. There is a choice of Ancient, Medieval or Modern Philosophy. She chooses Ancient because she thinks she will have enough background for that.

She attends her first lecture – it is on Plato's *Republic* and she is sure she will cope, having read the Penguin paperback edition of the Socratic dialogues after lights-out at boarding school under her blankets with the aid of a torch. The whole lecture is conducted in Ancient Greek. The students ask questions in Greek and read from their books in Greek. She doesn't understand a word. At some point, the professor notices that she is struggling and turns to her in Italian and kindly tries to include her by asking her about the South African republic. He asks her about the constitution. She remembers her embarrassment at having to explain that South Africa didn't have one. It is her first shuddering awareness of how limited her education has been.

She applies for a transfer to Modern Philosophy instead.

She meets a boy from Libya who is studying medicine in Bologna. Ahmed is his name. This is just after just after Qaddafi has come to power and has set up a bursary scheme for poorer students to study abroad.

Ahmed renames her; for the three or four years she lives with him she becomes Samira, no longer Anna. It is strange how happy she is to adapt and shift her identity to match other people's needs. When she thinks back, it seems to be something she has often done.

It bothers her a bit now. This question of names and naming and language. As if the label had no importance. As if there is a reality below language which is where she exists.

The room is completely silent. Suddenly afraid, she opens her eyes to see what he is doing.

129

He looks at her penetratingly, then smiles.

She closes her eyes again quickly.

She learns Quranic Arabic and applies to the Al-Azhar University in Cairo to study letters and is turned down because she is not Muslim. She feels relieved. She discovers Dante. And through him she hears echoes of Eliot shifting through herself. And she thinks of home for the first time. She asks the South African consul in Rome if her friend can apply for a visa to visit Cape Town. The consul explains that the application will have to go via Pretoria and that its success will depend on whether her friend looks dark-skinned or light-skinned in the photo. He explains that there is no automatic racial classification for Arabs; while the Chinese are coloured, the Japanese are honorary white, and the Turks are white, Arabs go on a case-by-case basis. She laughs.

She feels she belongs to his group of friends but she also feels excluded at the same time, because of course she isn't one of them and can't speak their language well, and they are all male – she is the only girl. They eat mbekbka nearly every night, sitting on the ground in a circle, and drum and clap and sing afterwards. They are treated with hostility by many Italians who call them *Turchi* or *Marocchini* and won't let them an apartment or trust them in any way.

She drives around with them at night, sitting in the back seat of the car with her face covered, to the streets where the prostitutes work. They take delight in asking the women the price of their services, but it never goes any further than that, at least while she is in the car.

Bologna is different from the Italy she has known until now. The people are dry, witty, practical, interested in reality and good food rather than mysticism. She attends lectures in the Faculty of Philosophy, but when she is free she also attends lectures in the School of Medicine with Ahmed. Everything interests her. She goes to an anatomy lecture and watches the professor and his assistants dissect a large bloated human body that is turning green and purple in places.

He sits forward, clears his throat and looks at the clock. She gets up.

Session 8

The usual room, the usual time.

It is a dark cold November evening in Milano. Shop lights reflecting dully, yellow and oily on the wet cobbles. Fog touching the skin, reaching up into the sleeves of her sheepskin jacket. She has come up from Bologna on the afternoon train and booked into a cheap *pensione* near the consulate, where she will go to write an exam the next morning, and has gone back out to find somewhere to eat. She peers into two restaurants but they look formal and expensive. Then she notices, across the street, between racing taxis, a *trattoria*. She crosses over and pushes open the doors. Warmth and good smells and a buzz of conversation spill out into the street.

She steps inside and looks around. Simple, unpretentious, but full. Every table is taken. On the far side she sees a woman sitting alone at a table, and, tired from the journey and reluctant to go back out into the cold, she crosses the room and asks if she would mind if they shared. The woman smiles and pulls out a chair. They fall into light conversation.

It feels like so long ago. But her mind is drawn back to that night, something about it unresolved still.

They chat idly, chance acquaintances in a big city. Then suddenly he arrives. She is embarrassed, an intruder, she motions to get up and leave them alone, they press her to stay. She stays. The conversation flows and ripples around the table, playfully, flirtatiously, she can feel the sexual undertow drawing her in; she allows it, curious to see where it will go. At midnight the *trattoria* closes, he invites the two women to his house for a drink, they exchange glances, accept.

The *portinaia* sticks her head out briefly as they stand waiting for the ancient lift to stagger to a halt on the ground floor, sees him, nods and withdraws. They laugh as the lift carries them up. They alight and he opens the door.

She wonders if it was the beauty of the apartment that made her stay. High ceilings, frescoes, walls covered with a dazzling collection of modern art – she recognises works by Modigliani, de Chirico, Guttuso, intermixed with rococo portraits of ancestors, a *monsignore*, a bishop – colours, shapes, insinuating, surrounding, holding. She realises she has unexpectedly walked into one of the most refined corners of the European intelligentsia. She feels the way Ali Baba must have when the door opened into the treasure cave.

She pauses a moment, thinking. Would she have found him so attractive if he had lived in an ordinary apartment and led an ordinary life? The question keeps bothering her, pulling at the edges of her consciousness.

They talk and talk. At last she tells them she must go. The invitation to go further is there, but she withdraws and it is fine. They accompany her back to her hotel.

When she gets back to her room she realises she has left her umbrella in his apartment. So after her meeting at the consulate the next morning, she goes back, expecting to find only the *portinaia* and hoping to be able to persuade her to recover the umbrella. But he is there, has taken the day off work.

He is delighted to see her and invites her in. Prepares a salad and omelette for their lunch. They sit in the kitchen with the scent of cooking in the air and drink wine from Orvieto, and the conversation meanders and they talk about art and politics, and he shows her the lithographs by Tono Brancanaro of the prostitutes of Padua, the *Belle del Prà*, whose eyes watch her knowingly. And he shows her the heavy oak armoire with the hastily scribbled message across the inside of the door – *Oggi il diciassettesimo giorno di novembre 1632 al tocco e mezzo è morto il parrocco, Don Luigi Sforza*. She agrees not to go back to Bologna until the next day so that he can show her around Milano. Late in the afternoon the woman, Laura, arrives from work. Somehow, over more food and wine and laughter, they find themselves in bed together. All three. She decides not to go back to

Bologna the next day either.

But eventually she has to leave.

He writes to her, long letters on green paper in green ink. She has never forgotten the strangeness of finding the green envelopes in her letter box covered in his spidery untidy handwriting. She checks the box several times a day. He writes that she must return. He tells her this meeting is something out of the ordinary. He mentions Nietzsche. *Al di là del Bene e del Male.* Beyond Good and Evil.

A few weeks later she travels to Paris and stops over in Milano to change trains. He is waiting for her at the station.

And now it is just the two of them. And a deeper undertow, something inexpressible, is between them, an intensity that seems to underscore every word. Often their eyes meet and hold. And he talks, about history, about his family, about literature, and she listens intently. He doesn't notice that she doesn't talk about herself. She mentions a boyfriend in Bologna. They leave the bed only to fetch some fruit, *panettone*, a glass of wine. He asks her to come and live with him. She agrees. They have met twice.

But back in Bologna Ahmed weeps and begs her not to leave, and eventually she gives in. And she sends a letter to Milan, calling it all off.

Those grey days after Christmas in the student apartment in Bologna. She wonders whether she has made a huge mistake. She tries to focus on the figure she is sculpting but her head is empty. There is a knock at the door, she opens. He stands there holding an enormous bunch of flowers in his arms.

She wonders why he has chosen chrysanthemums of all flowers. She's never liked them. The Italians call them *i fiori dei morti* – the flowers of the dead. Perhaps because they bloom in November when people visit their dead in the cemeteries.

He tells her he has come to fetch her. It is not a question. She can't say no. She packs a small overnight bag and her collected works of Shakespeare and leaves a note on the kitchen table for Ahmed:

'I am sorry. Goodbye.'

She leaves behind everything else, her motorbike, her books and records, her memories, her life.

She often wonders what she would have chosen to do if both he and Ahmed had stopped putting pressure on her and had left the choice to her. She thinks she would have gone with him. But she wasn't asked. So she has never made the choice.

She sighs.

And so she moves in with him. He knows nothing at all about her.

They walk out that first evening in Milano, around the Castello Sforzesco, in the misty cold night air. He tells her about the war, about how the Germans used to execute captured partisans up against the wall here in the moat. He shows her the bullet holes in the brickwork; she touches the tiny cavities with her fingers, softly, softly. Her threadbare corduroy coat is too light for this far north; she feels the cold creeping up her sleeves. He tells her about the Great Betrayer, *il Traditore*, Mussolini, his dead body hung upside down by the feet in Piazzale Loreto with his lover Clara Petacci. And the rawness of the fierce anger and hatred of the people of Milan.

She remembers how foreign and rootless she felt.

Thinking about it now, she realises he refashioned her to fit his needs. But she was happy to become whatever he wanted her to be. She had no clear idea who she was or what she wanted from life. She was willing to be moulded, shaped, like a ball of clay.

He tells her she will need clothes. They go to an atelier overlooking the Duomo where they sit on a sofa sipping wine while the assistants bring item after item for them to view. He selects four outfits.

– It's a start, he says.

He teaches her to cook, standing behind her to help her stir, his body cupped tightly against hers, like a limpet against a rock, while the scent of garlic and basil overwhelms her senses.

At times they feel like companions, like two male friends

out on the town. On one occasion they end up in a bordello and share a woman after the revelries of the night. They laugh. Nothing seems impossible. She would do anything for him, become anything he wanted.

Everything seems exciting, colours brighter than she has ever known them, flavours and smells overpowering. It feels like – and she supposes is, in a way – a very special life. He shares everything with her; she feels as if she would die without him.

She accompanies him on hunting trips to Hungary and Serbia and Bosnia and the Soviet Union. He makes her his bearer and she walks behind him carrying spare guns, ammunition, cognac. He gives her a bunch of leather thongs bound together on a hook to hang on her belt. Each thong ends in a tiny noose that fits around the necks of the birds he has shot. Ducks, geese, doves, blackbirds, songbirds, woodcocks, snipe. She feels the softness and warmth of the bodies brushing against her thigh as she walks.

She looks up. Outside the window, a starling lands on a branch and looks at her with its shiny black eyes, turning its head from side to side to scrutinise her.

The years in South Africa, the hospitals, the muteness feel like something from another life, remote. Yet of course they aren't. They are there, underlying it all. She knows that at some point she will have to tell him about her past. But it never seems to be the right time, and he doesn't seem at all curious to know about her. Of course she knows all about his childhood, and it is almost as if his memories have become her memories.

She stops to think. How is that possible? Memory is who you are. You can't have someone else's memories. But in a way she almost didn't exist.

Occasionally someone will ask her why she left South Africa, and she always struggles to answer. She has no words to describe what she has been through, and no understanding of it either. People often assume that there must be political motives behind her choice, but that feels untrue. She was not an activist and she is not in exile. Eventually she finds it easier to just avoid the question and pass for British. She looks British, her accent sounds English, and if anyone asks where exactly she comes from, it is easy enough to talk about London. But it feels like another level of falsehood. Another layer of confusion about who she is.

The longer she waits, the more difficult it becomes to tell him. And she doesn't know what she could tell him either that would make sense. She doesn't understand it herself. At some point it no longer feels possible for her to tell him about her past. The window of opportunity has come and gone. Even at this time of greatest intimacy, when it feels as if these moments of intensity will go on forever, when it feels as if they share everything, she finds she cannot. She needs to hide parts of herself that feel too raw, too shameful, too private, too vulnerable. And there is her deep need for privacy, her need to withdraw even from him. There is a level where he does not exist, where she cannot let him in, where she is totally alone. It is a perversely sexual, autistic sort of place.

There are little disappointments. Little betrayals. Slight rejections that feel unbearable, and then are forgiven. But not completely. So that a sensitivity to new rejections remains. She begins to withdraw, to fall more silent, each day a little further. Closing in on herself.

And then one day she summons the courage to talk, to tell him about her past. Oh, just little bits of it, not the whole story. She tells him about her father. She tells him about the psychiatric ward. She doesn't tell him about Luke, or the men in Rome. It is as if she has to show him that she exists. If she has a past, she exists. She isn't just an extension of his imagination. She thinks it might help him to understand, she thinks perhaps they will be able to recover the closeness they had once had.

But he feels cheated. He tells her he would never have taken her seriously if he had known. He says she must be mad.

One day they sit at the dinner table with friends, and she

sees him lift his finger to his temple and make that circular movement that means crazy, means mad, means *mal*, and point at her.

Perhaps she does go mad at that point. She could have tolerated anything else, but not that. She is not sure why. Perhaps she has always been afraid of that.

She packs an overnight bag, takes her collected works of Shakespeare, and leaves. For a while she wanders.

And then she comes to the island.

3
Book of the Future

You must give birth to your images.
They are the future waiting to be born.
Fear not the strangeness you feel.
The future must enter into you long before it happens...
Just wait for the birth, for the hour of new clarity.

Rilke

You can get lost in Tuscany without a map. Unlike the geometric grid of a South African landscape, where streets and roads cut straight across the countryside, here they meander and turn back on themselves and hesitate, passing by villages with strangely evocative names like Orgia and Saturnia, until you have no idea where you are going, nor know where is north or south, and barely can distinguish up from down. You feel disoriented. Lakes pass by on your left and disappear and a few minutes later reappear on your right. The roads wind steeply upwards around hairpin bends through woods of chestnut trees where wild boars and wolves have returned after half a century of absence.

It was the middle of winter when you left, *i giorni della merla,* the blackbird days as they call the bitterest, darkest days at the end of January. You found a bus, a *corriera,* to take you northwards, to Pitigliano, and then another on from there. You didn't bother to ask what its destination was.

You didn't talk, you and the boy. You bought two tickets, one for him and one for you, and you sat side by side on the hard seats looking out. You passed through the industrial outskirts of the city, and carried on past the lake of Bracciano under colourless skies with the smell of bonfires burning dead leaves and branches acrid in your nostrils. You don't know about him but you didn't see anything. The scenery passed in a blur. You were only aware of his small solid presence beside you on the bench.

First fallow wheat fields straggled along next to the road, interspersed with olive trees and vineyards that broke up as you began to rise into the hills and the woods closed in around you. The driver turned on the windscreen wipers as heavy raindrops began to splash themselves across the windows of the bus. The wipers seemed ridiculously small and only cleared a tiny section of the front windscreen. The windows soon misted up with the dampness so that shapes outside grew strange and contorted but neither of you tried to clear the mist from the glass. It reflected what was inside you – misty, dark, obscure.

141

At last you reached the final stop and you alighted. It was still raining, but the clouds appeared to be clearing in the west. You watched as the bus turned heavily in the little square, took on board its new passengers for the return trip, and, with a honking of its horn and a cloud of exhaust fumes, disappeared down the valley. There was a bar with a few tables stacked outside and a faded poster advertising Algida ice creams, but the door was locked, with rotting leaves piled high against it. It clearly hadn't been opened since the summer. Even the church was locked. You and the boy stood there. There was no one else around. You read the name of the village on the tattered bus timetable stuck on the notice board outside the bar – Serra. The fortress.

You wandered through the fortified village and stood for a moment high on the ramparts looking out over the forests, the valleys and gorges that reached to the horizon. It felt as if you were on the prow of a ship about to set sail into an ocean of brown leaves and spidery branches. You gazed out to the western horizon, where the sun was setting through black clouds. And then you lowered yourselves over the wall and dropped below the surface along a narrow path that wound its way downwards, you knew not where.

For days you walked through deep forests. Chestnut and plane and oak trees, deciduous trees, shady and soft, became your home. You shared this world with other shy silent creatures, foxes, ferrets, squirrels. One day a vixen accompanied you, curious, for several hours, trotting along parallel to you but a few arms' lengths away, stopping when you stopped, watching what you watched. Sometimes at night you heard snorting and rustling in the undergrowth, but the animals kept their distance, and all you encountered was their feral smell in the path, or spoor in the mud. Once at night you caught sight of yellow eyes staring at you and you knew it was a wolf. You froze and after a few minutes they disappeared. You did not tell Ugo for fear of frightening him, but you did not forget those eyes.

– Hurry, hurry, you said to him. We mustn't let anyone see us.

How long could you keep going? They were looking for you, you knew. You saw the newspaper headlines outside an *edicola* as you passed through a sleeping village by night. You saw your photographs side by side on the billboard, yours from your *permesso di soggiorno*, younger but recognisable by the deep haunted eyes and frown lines, Ugo's school photo taken a few years ago when he was much younger. No one had loved him enough to want to take or keep pictures of him more recently.

You fled from field to field, eating what you could, escaping, avoiding farmhouses and villages. A turnip here, tomatoes there, crusts of bread left out for the cats on another. You filled your pockets with ears of corn on one farm, where the farmer was unwise enough to plant his crop far from the watchful ears of his dogs. You gathered the last of the chestnuts, which you roasted over the fire at night on sticks, and mushrooms and the few remaining blackberries and blueberries, and when there was nothing else you sucked on stalks of wild sorrel or long stems of grass which you found in the occasional clearings between the trees. After a few days you were both very lean and your arms and legs scratched and bruised.

When you came to a small hamlet, often abandoned, the pickings were more abundant – the last apples off trees gone wild, walnuts fallen to the ground but still cold and sweet, vegetables gone to seed – and there was no danger of being caught. You sometimes slept overnight in one of the tumbled-down houses, but you were anxious about vipers and spiders, and the sense of despair and futility and loss in these places where once families had lived and prospered made you want to move on, to travel forward. You did not know where you were going, except that you must move forward.

And one day you came to the sea, to a long white strand with long white waves that mimed and echoed its forms. The child and you traced lines on the sand with your fingers and played noughts and crosses. He beat you every time and laughed uproariously when he did. He asked you to draw him a picture and you made a face with eyes but he didn't like that. He told you to draw him a dog and clapped his hands to see it. He asked you what its name was.

– Manfred, you said, it's Manfred.

– Tell me about Manfred, he asked, but you couldn't remember any stories to tell him and your mind just went blank each time you tried.

They were light-hearted days when you were still relieved at your escape, unconcerned about the future. You told each other stories as you walked, and sang songs and skipped stones off the sea. At night you gathered driftwood and made a little fire, and you hollowed out a soft shallow grave in the sand and lay down and sang lullabies until you fell asleep, and the stars above watched over you.

You came to a place where the cliffs rose up high and fell in a tumble of rocks into the sea, and you were forced inland if you wanted to continue. And it began to rain. The soft hushing sound of the rain, calling, inducing sleep, drowsiness, numbness in the brain, softening edges, smoothing, penetrating after so many days of enervating wind, of dryness and cracked, salty surfaces.

The shadow of an abbey fell across your path, with high solemn walls, an empty rose window above the altar, and no roof. The lead tiles that covered the nave had been used to make cannon balls for some war of dominion or other, perhaps the Napoleonic campaigns, perhaps something earlier, their significance long forgotten.

You stretched out on your backs on the grassy floor in front of the stone altar and gazed up at the night sky. You opened your arms wide on either side. Above you the universe was captured in the shape of a cross. Deep blue studded with sparkles of gold. Glowing, trembling with life, red stars, yellow, white, they sparkled in the cold brilliance of the night.

You watched, transfixed, a star shoot across the heavens from wall to wall. You half expected it to bounce off the far wall and ricochet backwards and forwards, ever downwards until it lay, vibrating, pulsating, gleaming on the tiny white flowers and grass that carpeted the floor of the abbey.

You came out at last, out of the low hills and valleys of the Maremma, forest-covered, with its steaming stinking sulphur springs, and radioactive mountains full of lead, and into the sloping wheatlands, the slow circles and bends woven by the plough over thousands of years. Where memory is held, is prized, is cherished, where the past is studied and revered, where history is in the bones of everything, where everything is named.

You sat on the edge of a lake, was it Bracciano, or Pitigliano, or even Trasimeno or Garda, and remembered the dry lakes of your childhood, the lakes of dust where there was no water. Just a borehole, a windmill, metal structure penetrating deep into the earth to tap into an underground stream, remnant of the waterways that once crisscrossed the plain. A bird soaring overhead. The dull, monotonous clanking of the borehole turned by the wind pulling up sullen brown *brak* water to the surface, unpleasant and salty to the taste, on the tongue; you had to be very thirsty to drink it, but one was always thirsty there. You remembered the place of your childhood, depleted, dry, barren.

A falconer stood at the edge of an open field, a bird on his gloved hand, hooded, like something out of a hieroglyph.

He waited.

The moment must be right. Then he slipped the hood off the bird's head.

He watched as the slow yellow eyes blinked, then blinked again, black pupils exploring the sky. As if in slow motion the wings opened and the claws released their grip and the body rose into the air, heavily at first. The wings thrust down hard against the pull, the suck of the earth, and then it was away, soaring high above the trees.

The falconer let it run, knowing that to try to call it in at this point would be fatal; the bird's will would be pitted against his and it would escape, probably for ever. He had to bide his time, allow it to stretch, allow it to sense freedom. Its own anxiety, not his, would bring it running back to check that he was still there.

When the falconer saw it return hurtling like an arrow towards him, he whistled *pwee* and gestured with his arm, and the bird wheeled and flew away again, but not so far this time. So when his shrill whistle came again *pwee pwee* the creature allowed itself to accompany him, to second him, to will what he willed, and it began to circle the field, at a distance first, far beyond the trees that bordered it, then the circles grew slowly tighter, smaller, the bird's head turning from side to side, its eyes watching the man on the ground, intrigued, held in his spell, not dominated but enthralled by him. At last the man pulled a dove from his bag, a dove half stunned, barely struggling, and showed it to the falcon, held it aloft, high in the air on his hand. The falcon slowed, circling lower now, closer, watching carefully, turning its head from side to side to gauge its prey. The falconer held up the dove, and then launched it high into the air.

With a smack the falcon dived and grabbed it in mid-air with its talons then soared up to the clouds, up to the heavens, in triumph, flying fast, winging swiftly up, up, escape, and freedom so close. And then the whistle, *pwee*, and again and again, *pwee pwee pwee*. The falcon could smell the blood, the warm flesh close to its own. The yellow eyes half closed for a moment, then the master's will took hold. The bird circled the field once more, and then descended and landed on his wrist and cast the dove at his feet. *Ptui*. It spat a few stray feathers from its beak, and then looked around shivering with wild eyes.

The man took the hood from his pocket and covered the bird's head affectionately, stroking the bony skull through the suede with the soft cushion of his thumb. He clipped the chain back onto the ring around the legs, then fed the falcon a piece of meat from his pocket. Not the quarry, not the prey. That was for him alone, the master. The bird had to learn to subdue its will to his. The man could make no mistakes in this game of domination and submission.

You stood in the shade of the trees, with the boy bedside you, watching. When he had finished you pulled back against the trunk and waited until he had disappeared into his battered car and chained the bird to a bar in the back of the vehicle. When he had driven away and over the crest of the hill in a cloud of dust and exhaust fumes you set off again across the field and into the woods.

At last you stop. You hadn't planned it that way, but there is no other choice. Ugo hurt himself this morning and can no longer walk.

You knew these abandoned buildings were dangerous. The floor collapsed under his weight and he plummeted into the cellar, cutting his thigh open on a metal spike, a deep, jagged gash. You try to clean it as best you can, with water from an outside cistern, but you have no bandages or disinfectant. You find a bottle of wine in a storeroom and a demijohn of oil. You pour some of the wine onto the wound but you don't think it will do anything. He does not even wince when it touches him. You tear off the sleeve of your blouse and bind that around his leg.

You are not sure whether he has just sprained his ankle or broken the bone. It seems to sit at a strange angle, but maybe he is just holding it like that because of the pain. He says he can't walk any further.

You tell him he must get up. You pull him up and hold him under the arms for support, but he cries every time his foot touches the ground. You don't know what to do. You pace up and down in despair.

But at last you are forced to give in and let him lie down again. You sit next to him for a while, but you keep thinking of dogs, of fierce dogs with snuffling noses, seeking, searching for you along the forest floor, tails wagging from side to side. But you know you will have to stop. You know you can't go any further.

It is a tiny hamlet, just a cluster of houses surrounded by a high stone wall hidden in amongst the trees. It looks as if it must have been abandoned decades ago, perhaps just after the war when so many people moved to the cities in search of work, and now nature has taken over. Weeds grow everywhere in abandon. Fig trees have sprouted and grown in cracks in walls, nettles collected below, pushing aside the bricks and stones until the wall falls at last and the house collapses. Roots buckle the cobbled alleys. You wander from house to house. Bats and pigeons have nested here over the years, leaving mounds of excrement and sticks and feathers and broken shells and bones piled high and smelly on the worn faded linoleum-covered floors.

There is a small square in the middle of the hamlet, an open space where the houses open out into a tiny piazza with a little chapel at one end and a boarded-up shop at the other. You imagine people sitting out here on a summer's night, talking and laughing and singing. It makes you feel very sad.

The main house looking on to the square is well proportioned, and is, like the others, built of grey river stones, but at one time it had been plastered and painted a warm ochre colour. It has withstood the assaults of nature better than the others. The rooms are dry and relatively clean.

The well in the square has a carved stone base depicting animals and flying birds around the rim. You drop in a stone and hear a clear plop as it hits the water. You put your head in and shout and the well shouts back again and again echoing your thin birdlike cry.

Pigeons roost on the wooden rafters of the little chapel or perch drunkenly on the faded triptych above the rotting altar. The roof has caved in, collapsed in one corner. Graffiti covers the walls beside the remains of a pew charred by the bonfire

148

lit by vagrants passing through; they have also defecated in the corners. There are the half-visible remains of frescoes on the wall, eroded, eaten away by damp and mould. Rain has almost washed the colours off two walls most exposed to the weather, but the paintings are still visible on the more protected walls. You can just make out the faded outlines of some figures, barely human any longer. You can make out bodies, figures falling, but you know you will need to clean them up and find a light to see them properly.

Lush weeds grow in the portico. You grab hold of one and pull it up by its roots. It gives you great pleasure to do so. It feels like coming home.

You have decided you will stay here for a while. Even if the boy weren't hurt you need somewhere to take refuge. Here you can sleep in front of the fire for as long as you like. You collect some firewood and light a fire in the huge fireplace in the kitchen. Upstairs you find an old mouldy mattress. You empty out the damp feathers and fill it with dry leaves and put it in front of the hearth where Ugo can lie down. You struggle to open the shutters and they give way at last and the golden sunlight pours in. You lean out. From where you stand you can see out over the tops of the trees. You can hear church bells rising through the clear air from far away. You can see the sprawl of Florence far off below you in a brownish haze, and at its heart Giotto's bell tower. There seem to be no other villages nearby but you are aware that curious woodcutters or shepherds might notice smoke coming from the chimney and come to see what is going on. But they would probably think it was just a vagrant who was passing through and wouldn't bother to check. Or so you hope.

And in the night you hear footsteps, and the sound of someone coughing – it sounds like a man. You and the child hold each other tight in the dark. And in the morning he is sitting in the square when you get up, with his back against the wall, warming himself in the sun. He looks at you blankly when you try to speak to him. You ask him if he would like some water. He smiles but doesn't say a word. Perhaps he is mute? He seems to see things that are not there and hears voices that only he can hear. He seems to understand when you speak to him in Italian, but he gets very confused, unable to do what you ask him.

When the sun is high he gets up and sets to work pruning the olive trees below the houses. He goes about the task with an easy rhythmic motion, as though it were something he had learned as a child. In the afternoon he returns and beckons you and Ugo to come to his house at the far end of the hamlet. Always in gestures. You follow him there. A woman stands framed by firelight in the doorway.

– Come inside, she says, your place is waiting.

You were taken in by Antonio and his sister Elisabetta, in their old house in the abandoned hamlet on the hill above the city walls, up the valley of the Torba, near to its confluence with the Ombrone, which flows down the hill through vineyards and olive groves to the plain. They took you in without any questions.

You went in and sat by the fire. The woman brought you a bowl of warm, scented water, round and whole, and a soft towel, and indicated that you should wash. She placed it on the ledge beside you. You plunged your hands in and splashed your face, feeling the dust and grime wash away. In the meantime she prepared a bath for you in the next room, which was filled with steam. You let yourself slip under the water, brushing the tangles out of your hair, washing your scratched aching body. The water felt soft and comforting. You almost fell asleep in the bath but managed to rouse yourself at the last moment and step out of the large tub. You wrapped yourself in the rough towel that lay ready for you on the chair, and combed out your hair in front of the fireplace. You felt reluctant to put on your dirty old clothes again, so you slipped into the homespun linen robe that had been laid out on the bed. You opened the door and the woman was there waiting for you; she took your hand and led you back to the kitchen and showed you to the table. You sat and she dished up steaming hot yellow polenta which Antonio cut with a piece of string. She laughed to see how hungry you were, and refilled your plate when you were finished. Ugo was smiling and seemed at ease in a way you had never seen before.

After dinner the woman sat beside the fire and sang songs that were strange and yet familiar at the same time. You listened to her singing and soon you realised you knew the songs and you joined in and sang with her, soft, sad songs of loss and grieving, and Ugo sang too.

At first you slept all day every day. Elisabetta tended to your needs and those of the boy, dressing his wound until it healed, so that each time you awoke she would be moving quietly about the room. You found you did not have the strength to rise from your bed, nor did you have the energy even to question why.

But you woke up one morning and the sun was shining through the deep-set windows of your room, and she called you to get up and sit by the fire. And you sat there with her shelling peas and listening to the sparrows chirping in the eaves.

And each day you grew a little stronger.

You went out with Antonio this morning. There was still frost on the ground and the *buozzo* was frozen over. He was pruning the olive trees in preparation for the new growth. Antonio did the work, you and the child walked behind raking up the cut branches into little mounds, which you set alight and left to smoulder in the crisp windless air. The smell of burning wood surrounded you as the small columns of smoke rose straight into the pale sky. You bent and straightened, feeling the muscles in your thighs and belly tighten and grow strong. The sun was barely bright enough to warm you, but the exercise created heat in your own body so that soon you were sweating. You felt a freedom and contentment you had not known for many years. When it was mid-morning Antonio shared his bread and olives with you and you sat on a log and looked out over the valley. All about there were little bonfires burning like yours. He traced out the limits of his land with a dirty finger, from the acacia on this side to the oak tree on the other. It had belonged to him and his family for many generations. He knew every tree and tussock intimately. He showed you where a fox had sunned itself early this morning on the path, miming its movements. And now you were back at work, working in tandem, tending to the exuberance of nature.

You looked out this morning and saw the young wheat springing up all around you, the first red poppies starting to flower, dancing on the ends of their long green stalks. You saw the first swallows of summer darting overhead, chasing invisible insects with shrill cries. You heard the low distant drone of a tractor and two men working on the far edge of a field, their attention completely focused on the task at hand.

There is an idea that has slowly been forming in your mind over these months in which your body has been idle. You would like to restore the paintings in the little chapel at the far end of the piazza. Antonio shows you a box of dyes and pigments that he has found in one of the abandoned houses and you set to work.

You have been here now for a year – you know because it is chestnut season again. You have made flour out of the chestnuts, and then *castagnaccio*, mixing the sweet brown flour with water and olive oil and then baking it in the wood ovens in large flat round trays. The year has gone around and now it is back to this. Back to the chestnuts, back to the *castagnaccio*. Antonio brings in loads of chestnuts and some you eat at once roasted in the fire and the others his sister puts out in the courtyard to dry in the late autumn sun, and then grinds to make flour. She has a kind of small mill off the kitchen.

The boy has grown tall in these months. He laughs often and helps Antonio with his work in the fields. You sometimes hear him whistling outside your window to imitate the birds of the woods as he works.

The leaves are falling in the woods behind the house. Golden red and brown they drift motionless in the still air, then spiral slowly down. There is a golden haze through the branches. Scent of mushrooms and myrtle. Sometimes you sit down where the rivers meet, the water eddies around as it rushes towards the sea. The seagulls, calling plaintively, come inland before a storm to take refuge.

When the winter is done it will be time for you to go. You have finished restoring the paintings. At Easter you will light the candles and allow everyone from the surrounding villages in. The priest will come and say mass in the little chapel. And when they have all gone you will pull on your coat and boots.

And you will open the door and slip out alone into the night.

Acknowledgements

I WISH TO EXPRESS MY ENORMOUS gratitude to the following people without whose support, love and guidance this book would never have happened: Athol Grieve, Stephen Watson, Imraan Coovadia, Paul Ashton, Ian Donald, Ursula Ulmer, Gill Mudie, Carrol Clarkson, Anne Schuster and Robert Bosnak. What you have each given me in your own singular way goes beyond words.

I wish also to express my thanks to AnnMarie Wolpe, Hillary and Tony Hamburger, Joan and Julian Leff, Carole Silver and Norman Levy whose enthusiasm and encouragement overcame my reluctance to publish this book.

Finally I would like to thank the jury of the European Union Literary Award 2013, as well as Jenefer Schute, Ester Levinrad and the editing team of Jacana Media who have made the intricate process of producing a book seem safe and easy.

The epigraphs on pages v and 1 are from TS Eliot's poem "Burnt Norton" from *Four Quartets*, published by Faber and Faber (London, 2001). The dictation Anna P gives her students on page 69 and 70 is from Robert Louis Stevenson's 1886 novella *Strange Case of Dr Jekyll and Mr Hyde*, originally published by Longmans, Green and Company (London), now available in various editions and in full at www.gutenberg.org. The extracts from Pontormo's diary are my own translations from the Italian, from the book *Diario Fatto Nel Tempo che Dipingeva il Coro di San Lorenzo (1554-1556)* by Jacopo da Pontormo, published by Gremese (Rome, 1988).